MIKE'S
OIL
PATCH

By
DORYS WARD

Illustrated By
J. Kay Wilson

Eakin Press ★ Austin, Texas

FIRST EDITION

Published in the United States of America
By Eakin Press
A Division of Sunbelt Media, Inc.

ISBN 0-89015-920-3

Library of Congress Cataloging-in-Publication Data

Ward, Dorys
  Mike's oil patch research / by Dorys Ward. Illustrated by J. Kay Wilson.
    p. cm.
  ISBN 0-89015-920-3
  1. Texas — History — Juvenile Fiction. [1. Texas — History — Fiction.
2. Oil exploration — Fiction.] I. Title.
PZ7.V934Co 1994
[E] — dc20

                                        94-2908
                                          CIP
                                          AC

Contents

Acknowledgments

Jan Artley, science coordinator, Midland Independent School District, Midland, Texas. Information on junior high and Expo '92 and the Science Fair in Midland.

Johnny Procell, employee of Salt Water Disposal Company in Kilgore. Information about salt water disposal and a tour of the pits.

Travis Thompson, tool pusher for Gibson Drilling Company. Tour of drill rig and explanation of how it worked.

Virginia Long of Long Trusts in Kilgore. Gave permission to use their name in the book.

Dan and Lynda Trent, dear friends and published writers who were always available for advice on writing and use of the computer.

Willard Chappell, district manager for Lufkin Industries, Inc., which sells pump jacks for the East Texas Oil Field. Checked accuracy of information on the pump jack.

Gina Baker, dear friend and Kilgore College English instructor, who helped me edit the manuscript.

CHAPTER ONE

The Research Begins

Sitting up a little straighter in the front seat of the truck, Mike Shannon looked ahead with interest at the newly graded road.

"Travis said to follow the graded road," Gramps remarked. "He told me they watered the road so there wasn't so much dust."

The road wound through the trees, and suddenly Mike saw the huge drilling rig in the cleared area. He could hear the motors and could see several of the men on the crew working on a platform. The platform sat on a steel supporting frame several feet off the ground. He saw ladders for the men to climb to get up on the platform. Lights were situated at various places so that drilling could be done at night. Several small red storage buildings surrounded the derrick. To one side, a metal supporting stand held long lengths of drill pipe.

A man wearing a green plaid shirt and a hard hat came toward them. Gramps shook hands and said, "Hello, Travis. Sure appreciate you letting me come out and bring Mike. This is my grandson." He nudged Mike forward.

As Travis shook hands, Mike felt almost grownup.

Travis explained the process of setting up a drill rig. "A well can be drilled on a forty-acre tract, but the lease can be much larger. We are going down sixty-two hundred feet to the Pulxay formation. Oil was found in the Woodbine formation in the first wells, but that formation doesn't produce here."

"How long does it take to get everything ready?" Mike wanted to know.

"About a week. We brought the derrick from Kilgore and set it up in one day. Putting the substructure or derrick floor together with pins is about a two-and-a-half or three-hour job. We have to level it up." Travis continued, "This is a self-standing derrick. That line over there is a climbing line for a derrick man."

The line he referred to was a heavy wire stretching from near the top at an angle to the ground. A weight attached to the line helped in the ascent of the man if there was trouble.

The crew was composed of a driller, derrick man, two roughnecks, and the tool pusher or supervisor, which was Travis' title.

Gramps pointed out the crown block, traveling block, hook, swivel, and the kelly that went into the rotary table. All these parts of the rig looked heavy.

Two platforms for safety were around the outside of the derrick. One was near the top and one about halfway down the steel frame.

Travis took them up on the drilling platform. Mike couldn't believe he was on a real drill rig—and such a big one. The noise grew louder, and Mike was fascinated as he watched the crew adjust the pipe that reached down in the drill hole. The drilling was done automatically with the use of a control box. Mike could imagine the bit biting away down in the hole. *How far is sixty-two hundred feet into the earth?* he wondered.

Gray water containing small rocks and other sediment was washing over a screen at the back of the rig.

"Mike, that's the mud," Gramps explained. "The drill bit rests on the bottom of the drill hole with the amount of pipe needed to get it there. With the bit on the bottom, the mud pump is started, and mud is forced down the pipe and through jet holes in the bit which is turning. The bit cuts

2

through rock or whatever is there, and these cuttings are carried back to the surface by the mud. The cuttings are what you see on the shaker or screen. The water goes through the mud screen into the slush pit, leaving the rocks there, and then the mud is recycled back through the drill casing."

A large pit had been dug at the back of the derrick for waste.

Climbing down off the platform, Gramps shook hands with Travis. "Thanks again for your time and trouble."

Travis turned to Mike. "Hope you learned something from this, Mike."

"Yes, sir." Mike shook hands with him.

Leaving the site of the drill rig, Mike asked, "Is that rig like the ones you worked on, Gramps?"

"Not exactly. They have a lot better equipment now and more safety features. Course, as the money from oil came into East Texas, there was money to spend on such things. Until the Woodbine showed the first traces of oil, Dad Joiner had to scrounge around for tools, parts, and labor. If he hadn't been so determined, things might have been different."

On the road again, Mike noticed they were taking a different route. "Where are we going now?"

"It's been a while since you saw the house where I lived when I started to work in the oil fields."

Almost hidden by trees, the small, white house was in fairly good condition. Mike looked at it with interest and tried to think what Gramps would have been like. He couldn't think of Gramps as ever being young.

The place looked deserted, and Gramps murmured, "I'll drive in and you can see the back of the place."

He slowly drove down the driveway, and as they rounded the edge of the house, a girl with long, blond hair ran onto the back porch with a disheveled man in pursuit. She ran into the yard, and before Gramps could stop the truck, the man swung at the girl. She ducked and he missed hitting her. The girl stumbled but didn't fall. Regaining her equilibrium, she raised her arms protectively around her head to ward off any other blows. Unsteady on his feet, the man hesitated to regain his balance.

Gramps stopped the truck and forgot his game leg in trying to get out and help the girl. He shouted at the man, "Hey, you, quit that!"

The man turned. Mike could see that his eyes were bleary. He seemed to have trouble focusing on the sound.

Drawing his mouth down in a hard, ugly line, he yelled, "Get off my place!"

Gramps, backed up by Mike, walked closer and put his hand on the girl's shoulder. He asked, "Are you hurt?"

The girl stood there without moving, but Mike could see her peeping at them under one arm.

The man glared, picked up a board from the ground, and with a noticeable limp started for Gramps. "I said," he repeated, "get off my place!"

Gramps backed up a little. Putting as much emphasis as possible into his words, Gramps told him, "Leave this girl alone."

Shaken, the man moved in front of the girl. Saying nothing, she slowly turned and made her way to the back door. The man, muttering to himself, followed her into the house.

Mike could tell Gramps didn't know what to do. They stood there in the driveway for a few minutes, stunned by the happenings.

A pickup truck pulled in beside Gramps' truck and a slim woman dressed in jeans and a blue blouse opened the truck door and got out.

Gramps moved quickly in her direction. He said in his most polite tone, "Howdy, ma'am. I'm John Shannon and this is my grandson, Mike." He paused for a moment to see the reaction of the woman. She didn't say or do anything.

Gramps tried again. "Do you live here?"

"Yes."

"I lived here many years ago in this house and stopped to show Mike the place . . ." He paused, thinking she might respond. Then he asked, "Is the girl related to you?"

"My daughter." Mike was beginning to think they weren't going to find out much.

"I don't know who the man is, but if that girl was my daughter, I wouldn't let her be around him." Gramps' tone became more belligerent as he remembered what had happened.

"Lisa gets out of line sometimes, like all kids." The woman didn't ask what had happened and apparently thought there was nothing more to be said. She turned back to the truck and took a small sack of groceries off the seat, slammed the truck door, and walked around them into the house.

"Guess there isn't anything else we can do, Mike." Gramps' shoulders drooped as he walked toward his truck. Mike followed.

They were quiet as they started back toward home. Finally, Gramps looked at Mike and said, "Think you learned anything?"

"Yes, sir."

Gramps evidently thought this was enough for the first trip to the oil field.

After supper was finished, Mike helped Gran clear the table and offered to dry the dishes.

Her hands deep in the sudsy water, Gran said, "Mike, this is one of my favorite times of the day. Gramps usually dries the dishes, and it's such a good time to talk. Now it will be a good time to share with you."

Gramps walked into the kitchen. "Mike, when you are through there, we had better talk over what else you want to see while you're here. Bring some paper out onto the patio, and we'll make a list."

Mike had come to Gramps' house in Kilgore for his summer visit, but this year would be different. He would be a seventh grader next fall, and his neighbor at home, a teacher, had suggested that he might want to participate in Expo '92 and the Science Fair. She said he could do some research in the summer and determine what he would build. Mike was taking advantage of Gramps' years as a roughneck in the oil fields to learn about oil. Maybe that could be his project.

Mike took paper to the patio table, and Gramps settled in the glider. "Let's see, today you saw the drill rig . . ." Gramps named different topics, and Mike made this list:

1. Drill rig
2. Geologic formations where oil is found
3. Dad Joiner and the Oil Boom
4. Oil Museum
5. Salt water pits
6. Pump jacks

Gramps thought for a while. "I guess that will do to get your project started. Let's forget oil for a while and watch the movie."

Mike took a shower after the movie. The girl hadn't been mentioned during the evening, but after he was safe in bed, the whole thing came back to mind.

Mike had roughhoused and wrestled with the guys many times, but he had never been struck by an older person. He saw again the arms of the girl held over her head to ward off any more blows. *Who was she, and who was the man? Didn't she have anyone who cared what happened to her?* Mike decided to talk to Gran in the morning.

He awoke early the next morning and lay in bed, watching the ceiling fan in the middle of the room revolve slowly. Gran turned the air conditioner off when they went to bed, and the soft whir of the fan had put Mike to sleep. Watching the blades turn, he again thought of yesterday and realized he had better keep some notes about the oil patch.

He rose from bed and settled himself at a maple desk with the paper containing last night's list. He would keep the notes in diary form.

Almost finished, he was aware of a soft knock on the door. He called, "Come in."

Gran stuck her head inside. Noticing the paper, she remarked, "You're busy for so early in the morning."

Mike stacked the sheets of paper in a neat pile and pushed it toward the back of the desk.

Gran seated herself on the edge of the bed, and Mike crawled back under the sheet and piled the pillows behind him. He looked at Gran and thought how proud he was to have her for his grandmother. Wearing a blue cotton robe that emphasized the blue of her eyes, she didn't look sixty. Gray hair curled softly around a face without wrinkles except for the network of laugh lines around her eyes.

Settling himself, Mike asked, "Gran, did Gramps tell you about the girl we saw yesterday?"

"Yes," she paused, "he was very upset and is trying to decide what to do about it." Gran's eyes mirrored her concern.

"What could we do?"

"Gramps knows a patrolman and will talk to him." Gran stood up and walked around to where Mike was sitting. She leaned over and kissed him on the forehead and said, "I'm glad you're here, Mike. Are you ready for breakfast?"

"Soon as I dress."

She turned and left the room.

Living in West Texas, Mike's family didn't visit here often. Each year, Gramps and Gran went to West Texas for Thanksgiving and stayed until after the new year, but Mike always came to Kilgore for a summer visit. From the past summers, Mike knew and liked several kids in the neighborhood, and he was anxious to see his old friends.

Gramps wanted some help with yard chores, and it was later in the morning before Mike went out into the street.

A boy on a ten-speed bike rode toward him. The boy was darkly tanned with sun-bleached hair. It took Mike a few minutes to recognize Jeremy Scott. Mike didn't remember Jeremy as being so tall.

Jeremy screeched to a halt and laid the bike on the curb. Running toward Mike, he grabbed his arm and said, "Hey, man, good to see you. I heard you were coming and looked for you yesterday when I delivered the paper." Jeremy's blue eyes shone with friendliness.

Putting his arm around Jeremy, Mike said, "Gramps and I went to see a drill rig. Ever been on one?"

"No, why? Were you on one?"

"This year, Goddard—"

"Goddard?" Jeremy interrupted.

"My school, Goddard Junior High."

"Don't you have a middle school?"

"No. Seventh grade is junior high at home. Anyway, there is something new this year called Expo '92. We display our Science Project there the last of February and then again at the Science Fair on April 4."

Jeremy seated himself on the curb. Mike sat beside him.

"Have you entered before?"

"No, not anything like this. It'll take a lot of work. That's why I need to get information this summer."

Looking at Jeremy's tan, Mike asked how he go so brown.

"I started delivering papers after my eleventh birthday, and Mom bought a season pass to the swimming pool. I go swimming every afternoon. Can you go today?"

"I'll ask Gran."

As the boys started up the street, in the direction of Bobby Burton's house, Mike asked, "Do you think Bobby is up yet?"

"I don't know. He watches TV a lot and stays inside."

Bobby walked out into the garage as the boys came up the driveway. Barefooted and wearing a pair of rumpled shorts, and heavier than Mike remembered him, he led the way into the house.

An old movie playing on the TV screen and a dish of macaroni and cheese on the floor beside two sofa pillows indicated the way Bobby spent much of his time. A German shepherd lay by the dish of macaroni. Her head resting on her paws, she glanced up but didn't move.

"I made macaroni and cheese. You guys want some?" Bobby offered.

Jeremy looked at his watch. "I have to go and make sandwiches for me and Mom. She'll be home for lunch."

For a while the boys watched the movie, an old Western with John Wayne.

Jeremy said he had to leave and, turning at the door, he again asked, "Mike, do you want to go swimming?"

"I'll ask Gran and call you."

"What about you, Bobby?"

"The pool is too crowded. The only place I swim is in Sam Rice's pool, and he's on vacation." Bobby's eyes returned to the TV screen.

"See you guys later," Jeremy said as he left.

For the second time, Bobby offered macaroni.

"It looks good, but Gran is expecting me."

"You guys are something else. You have to eat with your grandparents and Jeremy has to eat with his mom . . ." He dug into the macaroni.

"Does Jeremy's dad come home for lunch?" Mike asked.

"They got a divorce. Now Jeremy thinks he has to be there for his mom. He even has to leave a note on the table when he leaves the house."

Mike mentioned the girl they had seen yesterday.

"Where does she live?"

Mike tried to remember how they came back to Gramps' house yesterday. "Out 42 Highway, I think."

"I don't know her, but a girl something like that came into one of the other fifth grades last year. I think her name was Lisa Jacobs."

"Jacobs! That's it — that's the name on the mailbox." In the excitement of yesterday, Mike had forgotten the name. He wondered if Gramps knew.

At lunch, Mike asked Gramps if he knew the girl's name and Gramps said, "Yes, Charles Butterworth told me her name."

"Butterworth?" Mike looked at Gran.

"He's the policeman Gramps talked to about Lisa," she said and turned away.

Mike looked from one grandparent to the other, but neither offered any further information.

Mike swam with Jeremy that afternoon until time for

Jeremy to run his paper route. In the evening, he and Gramps watched the Rangers' baseball game on TV.

Mike didn't realize it at the time, but Lisa would be another very important topic added to his summer's research.

CHAPTER TWO

Discoveries at the Library

The phone rang next morning before Mike finished his chores. Jeremy wanted to know if he could go bike riding.

"I don't have a bike here."

"We have an extra one," Jeremy said.

"Okay, I'll come to your house."

Searching for Gran, Mike found her on her knees pulling grass from the shrubs along the front walk. She rose to her feet, stretched, and said, "Sure hard on my back."

"Jeremy wants me to go bike riding, Gran. Be back before long."

"Be careful, and don't be late for lunch."

Jeremy lived two blocks down the street. When he saw Mike, he walked out to meet him. Jeremy's red ten-speed and another blue one almost like it were in the garage.

"Which one do you want to ride?" he asked.

"Is the blue one yours too?" Mike looked it over.

"No, it belonged to Dad. We rode together sometimes. Mom had one, too, but she sold it after Dad left."

"Why did your dad leave?" Mike hated the thought of Jeremy being without a father.

Mike noticed Jeremy's eyes cloud over. He quickly turned toward the back door, and Mike could scarcely hear him when he said, "My library book's due. I'll get it." He went into the house.

Jeremy didn't mention his dad when he came out with the book under his arm. He merely said, "Mom makes me pay the fine if there is one. Let's go to the library first."

Mike loved the feel of the wind on his face as they rode in and out of the shady areas along the streets. Leaving the bikes in a rack near the library door, they went inside.

Jeremy walked to the checkout desk and Mike suddenly remembered his research. This would be a good time to look up geologic formations.

There was a computer in the library to locate books. Mike read the instructions, pushed the right keys, and soon had several books listed on the screen. Searching in the stacks, he found several books on oil. He sat down at one of the tables to see if there was information about the areas of earth where oil is found.

Thumbing rapidly through the books, Mike realized he already knew some of the information. He knew that the formation of the earth where oil is found began as long as 750 million years ago. Tiny plants and animals died, and some parts of the decayed material formed tiny particles of oil and gas. These tiny drops would later be found in layers of rock. The layers, squashed by mud and sand from rivers, were forced into spaces between grains of sand. Some of the mixture was pushed into hard rocks called shales. Oil was found in shale.

Mike read that the shells of tiny sea animals decomposed and made limestone along the shores. Oil was found in limestone.

Over millions of years, the earth heaved up and formed anticlines. Oil and gas had moved up within the layers of sand where it was trapped. Earthquakes changed the face of the earth and affected the oil pockets.

Jeremy had checked out another book and brought it to the table. It was a big book, simply titled *The Earth*. Jeremy laid it on the table and began to turn the pages. Noticing the many colored illustrations, Mike became interested.

The origin of the earth, how it formed, different periods of development from no life at all to the present — all these were discussed and illustrated.

Totally engrossed, Mike didn't notice the girl when she first came into the room. Turning a page, he happened to glance up and see Lisa. Wearing a green shirt and shorts, she walked slowly along the shelves, taking out a book here and there.

Mike didn't know what to do. He wanted to ask her if she was all right.

She selected several books and walked over to another table, where she seated herself with her back to Mike and Jeremy.

Mike rose. Jeremy, thinking Mike was ready to leave, stepped in behind him. Mike gently pushed down on his shoulder. "Wait a minute," he said very softly.

Lisa didn't look up as Mike came to her table. Keeping his voice low, he began, "Hi . . ."

Lisa glanced at him. Mike thought how pretty she was, and he couldn't remember ever seeing eyes so green.

"Oh, hi." She looked back down at the open book.

Mike sat down. "Are you all right?" She didn't answer, so he tried again. "Gramps and I worried about you the other day — you know, when your dad tried to hit you. We were parked in the driveway where you live . . . Gramps lived there . . ." He struggled to find words.

Ignoring him and with her eyes lowered, she turned several pages.

Mike waited for a few minutes. What was the matter with her? Guess she didn't want to talk. He became angry and started to leave.

Lisa looked up and, speaking in a whisper, said, "He isn't my dad."

Mike sat down again. "Who is he?"

"My stepdad."

"Is he mean to you?"

"Sometimes . . . if he's been drinking."

"Does your mom know?"

"Yes, but she says to keep out of his way. He has problems of his own."

"What kind of problems?"

Mike didn't notice, but Jeremy had moved to a closer table.

"My dad and Bob, my stepdad, were hurt in the crash of a Medivac helicopter. Daddy died."

"And Bob?" Mike questioned.

"He has a bad leg and takes a lot of medicine to kill the pain. Mom says that's why he drinks."

"Does he work?"

"No, not now. He and Mom had a trucking business, but it went broke. Now Mom has lost her job. She's worried about bills."

Mike couldn't think of anything to say. He just sat there. Others came into the room, and Jeremy came over to stand behind Mike. "We'd better go, Mike,"

Still speaking softly, Mike asked, "Would it be all right if Jeremy and I rode out to your place sometime? Oh, this is Jeremy Scott."

Glancing at Jeremy, Lisa's face brightened, and she said, "Hi, Scotty."

Again, Mike asked, "Could Jeremy, uh, Scotty, and I ride bikes out to your place?"

Lisa looked at Jeremy and smiled. "If Bob doesn't catch you."

Riding slowly homeward, Jeremy, or "Scotty," remembered he had to make lunch.

Later, Mike went to his room to add to his notes. Sitting at the desk, he thought about Lisa. He had parents who cared for him, and he suddenly realized other kids weren't so lucky. Bobby, Scotty, and now Lisa had problems. Mike didn't know what could be done, if anything.

And he didn't know how he felt about Lisa being so interested in Scotty.

CHAPTER THREE

Goin' Fishing

Mike opened his bedroom door next morning and could smell bacon. Gran placed a plate of bacon, toast and two eggs, sunnyside up, in front of Gramps as Mike walked into the kitchen. Pointing to another chair at the table, Gramps said, "Gran has already poured your orange juice. Tell her how much breakfast you can eat."

"Same as Gramps." Mike took a long drink of juice.

Soon Gran placed a plate in front of Mike. Wiping her hands on a towel, she said, "I'll have to go and get ready for my job."

Between bites, Gramps explained they would have to help with cleanup because Gran worked at the Oil Museum as a docent.

"What's a docent, Gramps?"

"In Gran's case, it's a person who takes groups through the museum. Many out-of-town visitors come for tours, and during the school year buses bring schoolchildren. Keeps 'em busy."

Gramps pushed his plate to one side and asked, "What do you want to do today?"

"How long will Gran be at the museum?" Mike took the last piece of bacon.

Gramps' eyes twinkled. "It's her day out. She works 'til

16

noon, eats lunch with a friend, and they spend the after-noon doing whatever women do when they get together."

Taking a last sip of coffee, he suggested, "We might eat lunch at McDonalds."

"My favorite place."

Later, as Gramps parked at the museum to let Gran out, she asked Mike to walk her to the door. She took his arm, saying, "It's not every day I get to walk on the arm of a hand-some young man."

Mike noticed three large figures to the right of the front door. Surprised, he asked, "Who's that?"

"Dad Joiner, Doc Lloyd, and Daisy Bradford. Gramps can tell you about them." Mike opened the door and Gran went inside, saying, "I'll see you this afternoon."

Back in the car, Gramps asked Mike if he would like to go fishing. "Sometimes fish bite in the late afternoon."

"Where do you go?"

"There's a lake in Windom's pasture. You haven't been there, but I've known old Jess for years, used to work with him. He's living with his son now, and the pasture is on their place. They told me I could fish in the lake. I've caught some good perch there at times."

At the house, Mike joined Gramps in the backyard, where he was digging for worms in Gran's compost pile. Mike picked up the fat, pink worms and put them in the can partly filled with dirt.

Gramps went to the garage closet and took out several pieces of fishing gear. "Do you want a rod and reel or a cane pole, Mike?"

"Rod and reel."

"We'll get washed up and go and eat lunch. Have some time to rest afterwards."

Taking the lunch tray to a table at McDonalds, Mike began to eat his chicken nuggets. He remembered the figures at the door of the Oil Museum.

"Gran told me you knew about Dad Joiner and Doc Lloyd?"

"Let's wait and talk at the house, since it is a long story."

They didn't get to talk because Bobby and another boy were sitting on the curb in front of Gramps' house.

Mike approached them, and Bobby said, "Mike, this is Sam Rice."

"Hi, Sam." Mike saw a boy smaller than Bobby with very black hair and black eyes. He also saw a very expensive BMX bike leaning against the curb.

Sitting down on the other side of Sam, Mike became aware of Sam scooting his foot back and forth slowly. He wore a pair of new Michael Jordan shoes.

"Sam asked me to swim this afternoon—" Bobby began.

Sam interrupted, "In my pool."

Bobby continued, "Can you go?"

"Gramps and I are goin' fishing. I could go before then." Turning to Sam, he asked, "Where do you live?"

"It's about three blocks. We can walk."

"Let me tell Gramps and get my suit." Mike started toward the house. He turned and added, "I'll have to be back to go with Gramps."

Mike understood why Bobby liked Sam's pool. No one was home, and they had the pool all to themselves.

Later, wearing his swim trunks and with a towel hanging around his neck, Mike walked back alone because Sam and Bobby were going to play some video games on TV.

Gramps was waiting in the front yard. Mike hurried and changed into some jeans and a pair of old sneakers. He walked into the garage to see Gramps loading the rod and reel and two cane poles with attached fishing lines and hooks into the truck.

"We'll leave Gran a note. No telling when she will get tired of her day out." Gramps left the note on the kitchen table.

The lake wasn't far from Gramps' house if they had walked, but by road it took a little longer.

Gramps turned off the main road onto a private driveway. A large overhead sign spanned the drive, and on it Mike read "W BAR W RANCH." The truck rumbled over a cattle guard beneath the sign.

Mike saw a low ranch house surrounded by trees and shrubs on the right-hand side of the drive. Ranch outbuildings were clustered together a short distance from the house.

Gramps slowed down and looked as they passed the house. "Don't see anyone. Jess said to go on in anytime, so I guess it's all right." He followed the drive back of the house down to the lake and parked under a huge oak tree.

Mike saw a small, flat-bottomed boat beached on a wide gravel bar. The graveled area extended fifty feet or more down to the water. Mike jumped from the truck and ran over and grabbed Gramps' arm. "What a neat place to camp out!"

Gramps said, "You'd have to ask Jess, son."

Gramps picked up some of the gear. "Let's go around to the west side. Shadier there."

They walked up on a dam and around to the west. Mike had never seen anything prettier. The sun, sliding toward the western horizon, cast a reflection of the trees into the water. A brisk southern breeze ruffled the water, making the images shimmer.

Gramps baited the hooks on the two cane poles, and Mike did the same with the rod and reel. Gramps stuck the end of one pole into the soft mud along the bank and settled down with the other pole in his hand.

Mike walked up and down the bank, casting with no success. Gramps caught a nice perch weighing about half a pound and soon pulled in one a little larger. He threaded the fish on a stringer and put them in the water, anchoring the metal end of the stringer securely along the bank.

Mike decided to try a cane pole. In a short time, the cork was pulled under and the fishing line pulled tight.

"Play it easy," Gramps cautioned.

Mike landed a perch, not too big, but large enough to keep.

They fished until the sun disappeared. Gramps began winding up the fishing line on his cane pole. "Better go home or Gran will be worried."

Mike wound up the line on the other pole and picked

up the rod. Back at the truck, Mike again mentioned camping out. All Gramps said was, "We'll see."

Surprised at the nice string of fish, Gran suggested having a fish fry the next evening.

After supper, Mike helped clean the fish, took a shower, and went to bed.

CHAPTER FOUR

Finding Answers

Mike added a few notes to the research pages the next morning before leaving his room. Eating a bowl of cereal with skim milk, Gramps looked up as Mike slid into a chair at the kitchen table. Pointing to the cereal, Gramps said, "Had my eggs for the week. Gran makes me watch cholesterol. You can have anything you want. That is, if we have it."

"Cereal is okay. I'll get it."

Pouring the cereal into a bowl, Mike asked, "Where's Gran?"

Gramps smiled. "Resting up after a hard day yesterday with the girls."

Gramps would clean up the kitchen, so Mike made his bed and went into the yard. Jeremy was coming down the street.

Walking out to meet him, Mike asked, "Do you really want to be called Scotty?"

"Yeah. I like it. Have to get Mom to call me that too."

"Scotty, what's on your mind?"

"Can you ride out to Lisa's?"

"I don't know. Maybe we could go riding and just happen by her house. How far is it?" Mike wasn't sure Gran would want him to go that far, but he really wanted to see Lisa again.

"She lives at the edge of town. I go by her house on my paper route."

"Isn't it out 42?"

"You can go that way."

"Do you know her?" Mike hadn't realized Scotty already knew Lisa.

"I see her sometimes in the yard. We'll both be in middle school this year. She's a year behind me."

"I'll tell Gramps we're going bike riding."

Pedaling slowly along the streets, Scotty led the way. Lisa's house was closer than Mike remembered.

The place looked deserted when the boys rode up the driveway, but Lisa's mother came out the back door onto the porch as they rounded the corner of the house. Both boys stopped and sat there.

Looking from one to the other, she questioned, "Do you want something?"

Encouraged that she had at least spoken, Mike said, "We came out to see Lisa. Is she home?"

"Yes, Lisa is home. I'm Lisa's mother, Trish Jacobs." She stepped to the door and called, "Lisa, someone here to see you."

Mike didn't realize until then how apprehensive he had been about coming here. After the treatment he and Gramps experienced on the last visit, he wasn't expecting anything better this time.

Lisa appeared in the doorway. Seeing the boys, she came outside. Barefooted, she wore a pair of cut-off jeans and a blue tank top. Shyly, she said, "Hi."

Trish started back into the house and then paused. "Lisa, why don't you ask the boys to come inside? The cookies are almost done."

Mike and Scotty stood the bikes against the back porch railing and followed Lisa into the house.

The smell of baking cookies permeated the small kitchen. Sparsely furnished, the room was spotlessly clean. Lisa led the way into a room which had a portable TV, a sofa, and several easy chairs. There were many photographs on a table in the center of the room.

No one spoke. Scotty and Mike sat on the edge of two of the easy chairs. Finally, Lisa picked up one of the photographs and said, "This is my dad."

22

A handsome man in the uniform of a pilot in the U.S. Air Force smiled back at them from the snapshot. He was standing beside a helicopter. "That was taken in Vietnam," Lisa explained.

Placing the picture back on the table, she took up another. "This is Dad and Bob when they were working as a Medivac team."

Mike would never have recognized Bob from the photograph. There was no resemblance to the man he and Gramps had seen on their last visit here.

Trish came into the room with a plate of warm cookies and some iced tea. The four were silent as they slowly munched on the cookies.

Evidently, Trish thought an explanation of her behavior last time was necessary. She began, "I want Lisa to have friends, and it is nice when they come to see her —" She stopped and then tried again. "Things at our house are not always good." She seemed to be searching for the right words.

"You see, Bob is not well. He has gone to the VA hospital now for treatment on his leg. It pains him a lot, and he has become addicted to the drugs he takes." Her eyes lowered to hide her distress.

"It hasn't always been like this. The three of us were a happy family and Bob a best friend. After Ron's death and Bob's injury, the bad luck has piled up, and I know it's been hard on Lisa. I'm hoping we can work it all out, some way."

Lisa rose and went to her mother. Hugging her, she said, "It's okay, Mom. It'll all work out."

Mike and Scotty sat there in silence. To Mike it didn't seem fair that people should have so much bad luck.

Scotty shifted uneasily in his chair several times. Finally, he stood and asked, "Are you ready to go, Mike?"

Trish and Lisa followed them to the door. Trish held out her hand. "I'd like to ask you to come back, but I know it isn't always possible when Bob is in one of his bad moods. He doesn't mean to be cruel. He really needs treatment for all his problems. I am trying to get him to go to a VA hospital for psychiatric counseling."

Putting her arm around Lisa, she added, "It disturbs me when he mistreats Lisa, and something will have to be done about it soon."

The boys rode back to Scotty's house. Mike wheeled the bike into Scotty's garage.

"See you later," he called.

Gran had fixed a lunch plate for Mike and said they were eating out on the patio. Settled at the table, she looked at Mike. "Did you have a good morning?"

Before thinking, he answered, "Scotty and I rode out to Lisa Jacobs' house." He glanced quickly at both grandparents to get their reaction.

"Scotty?" Gran didn't recognize the name.

"Jeremy, Gran. He wants to be called Scotty."

Neither said anything about Mike riding so far, but Gramps asked, "Did you see *that* man again?"

"No. He's gone to the VA hospital. He's Lisa's stepdad." Mike ate half a sandwich and said, "Her mother's real nice, Gramps."

Gramps took a drink of iced tea. "She didn't act nice to me."

"They've had a bad time. Lisa's dad was a helicopter pilot in Vietnam. Bob was his navigator, and they worked as a Medivac team until their 'copter crashed."

"How awful." Gran laid down her fork. "What happened to Lisa's dad?"

"He was killed." Mike continued, "Now Lisa's mom has lost her job, and the unemployment has about run out."

Gran shook her head. "Sounds like a lot of trouble."

Gramps pushed back his chair. "Bob is Lisa's stepdad?" Mike nodded.

"He's a mean acting dude," Gramps said.

"Trish, Lisa's mother, says it's his leg."

"That's no reason for being mean to Lisa." Gramps wasn't buying the excuse.

Gran started to clear the table. "Maybe we don't know the whole story."

CHAPTER FIVE

Dad Joiner's Story

Lunch things cleared away, Gramps asked Mike if he had plans for the afternoon.

"No, why?"

"You wanted to know about Dad Joiner and Doc Lloyd. We can talk now."

"Okay."

Settling into the patio glider, Gramps leaned back and began. "His name was Columbus Marion Joiner. He was born in 1860 in Alabama, and by the time he was eight both his parents were dead. An older sister raised him, and he learned to read using the Bible's Book of Genesis."

Gramps pushed the glider for a few minutes. "Dad left home when he was seventeen and wandered through the South. He married, ran a store, studied law. His sister married a Choctaw Indian, and this led him to the oil fields. He supervised the leasing of Indian lands to white farmers."

Gramps quit talking when he heard the whir of a hummingbird's wings. The tiny bird flew to the red feeder and daintily put its long bill into the little cups to sip the sugar water. Satisfied, it flew away.

"Around 1907, Dad met Doc Lloyd. Lloyd's real name was Joseph Idelburt Durham."

"Why didn't he use his real name?" Mike asked.

"He was a ladies' man and didn't want ladies he had known to be able to find him."

"Oh, that kind, huh?"

"Doc Lloyd worked at many things. He had been a chemist, druggist, mining engineer, prospector for gold in the Yukon and Mexico. He had a medicine show and traveled around and sold medicine." Gramps used his fingers in listing all of Doc Lloyd's so-called professions. He spoke slowly, pausing often in trying to remember all he knew.

"Dad and Doc were really adventurers. They joined up in buying and selling oil leases and nearly hit oil several times. The two separated, and Dad moved to Rusk County in 1926. Around 1927, he located Doc Lloyd and brought him to Overton. They got a lease on 970 acres on Daisy Bradford's farm. They spudded in—"

"What's 'spudded in' mean, Gramps?"

"Started drilling. The first well was drilled in 1927. In April of 1928, the number-two well was started. After eleven months with no success, they shut down."

"Why?"

"Worn out equipment and lack of money."

"Did they quit?"

"No. They started to pull the drill rig to a new location, but a sill supporting the derrick caught on a rock and broke. There wasn't money to buy a new sill, so they drilled there and struck oil."

The little bird returned to the feeder. Again, Gramps waited before continuing the story.

"The well was named the Daisy Bradford Number Three. It brought hundreds of people to Kilgore and opened the East Texas Oil Field. Daisy Bradford is the woman with Doc and Dad in the Oil Museum."

"When did you come here, Gramps?"

"My folks moved here in 1939 from Missouri. My dad needed work. I joined the army and didn't get back home until 1945, when I got a job in the oil fields."

"Did you know Gran then?"

"Met her in 1948. She was seventeen years old and a senior in high school. Cutest thing you ever saw, Mike. For that matter, she still is."

Coming out onto the patio, Gran heard the last remark. She placed her hand on Gramps' shoulder and, patting him, said, "Don't believe everything he tells you, Mike."

Gramps yawned and got up from the glider. "Let's stop for now. I need to take a short nap," he said.

Smiling at Mike, Gran shook her head.

Mike went to his room to add to his notes. He didn't know it then, but later in his life he would follow to a certain extent in Dad Joiner's steps. His search would be for a different source of energy — pollution-free energy.

CHAPTER SIX

A New Friend

Mike didn't see Gramps around when he came from his room. Starting to the side door, he heard Gran call softly, "Mike."

He stopped. "Where are you, Gran?"

"In the kitchen. Did you forget we were having a fish fry tonight?"

"No. Why?"

"I thought you might like to ask some of the boys for supper. We have enough fish."

"Who?"

"You choose."

"What time, Gran?"

"About six."

"I'll go and ask Scotty."

Mike saw Scotty come out of the garage, an empty paper satchel hung on his shoulder. Seeing Mike, he grinned. "You're in time to go with me to deliver papers."

"I can't today but I will later. Can you come and eat supper at Gran's tonight?"

"Sure. I won't have to eat by myself. Mom works late. What time?"

"About six."

"I'll hurry."

Mike found Bobby and Sam watching stock car races on

TV. When the commercial came on, he asked, "You guys want to eat fish at Gran's tonight?"

Sam looked up. "We're supposed to go to the ballgame."

"Could you eat first?"

"I guess so. Mom will pick us up in time for the game. Okay with you, Bobby?"

"Yeah. I love fish."

"See you both about six," Mike said, opening the back door. He saw a freckled boy with red hair and brown eyes standing there.

Grinning, the boy asked, "Is Bobby home?"

"They're watching stock car races."

The boy paused in the doorway. "You're Shannon's grandson, Mike. Right?"

"How did you know, and who are you?"

"B. J. Elliott. My folks and I moved in last month over on the next street. Bobby said you always come to visit in the summer. How long you been here?"

"A few days."

"We've been on vacation. I hate it. Riding in a car with nothing to do." Nervously, he ran his hands through his hair.

On impulse, Mike asked, "Want to eat fish at Gran's tonight?"

"If Mom will let me."

"About six, if you can come. See you later."

Gran served plates of crisp brown fish with hush puppies, French fries, and slaw. With her eyes she counted boys so there would be the right number.

Sam picked at his plate and ate little. Bobby ate all his food and asked for seconds. B. J. and Scotty were nearly finished when a car honked.

Sam jumped up, nearly upsetting his chair. "That's Mom."

Bobby stuffed the last few bites in his mouth and mumbled, "Thanks, Mrs. Shannon. Really good."

The other boys thanked Gran, and she followed them to the front door. The motor purring softly, a large white

Cadillac stood in the driveway. A black-haired young woman sat at the wheel of the car. She rolled down the window and called to gran, "Thanks, Mrs. Shannon, for feeding the boys. I'm Sam's mother."

"Glad to have them." Gran turned to Mike. "Do you have money, Mike?"

Sam's mother overheard Gran. "He won't need any. My treat."

Arriving at the ballpark, she gave each boy $5. "There's no admission charge, and this should pay for soft drinks."

The last half of the fifth inning, Mike said he wanted a Coke. Sam, on his second hamburger, munched away, and Bobby indicated he was full. B. J. and Mike left the bleachers for the concession stand. Waiting in line, B. J. turned to Mike. "You're lucky, Mike."

"Why?"

B. J. lowered his voice. "You can visit with your real grandparents."

"Can't you?"

"I don't know who they are."

"How come?"

"I'm adopted. My folks think I don't know. They try to make me believe they're my real parents." B. J. looked around while confiding as though he might be ashamed.

"How did you find out?"

B. J. spoke barely above a whisper. "One night I started for the bathroom when they thought I was asleep. I heard Mom say, 'We need to tell B. J. he's adopted.' "

"What did your dad say?"

" 'We can tell him later. Just leave it alone.' "

Stepping up to the counter, the boys ordered Cokes. B. J. didn't mention his parents again.

Watching a late movie, Gran looked up when Mike came into the house. She yawned. "It's getting late for an old lady. Have a good time? Did our team win?"

"I had a good time. Our team lost."

Mike rattled some coins in his pocket. "Did you have enough money?" Gran asked.

"I bought a Coke and gave most of the money left over to Sam. Gran, he ate all the time we were there!"

"Maybe he doesn't like home cooking. I noticed he didn't eat much."

Mike said goodnight and went to his room. Sitting on the side of the bed, he wondered how it would feel not to know his parents.

CHAPTER SEVEN

A Happy Fourth for Scotty

The town went all out on the Fourth of July — a parade in the morning, contests of various kinds all day, a large carnival set up in vacant lots with concession stands selling different varieties of food, a band concert in the evening, and fireworks about 10:00.

Sam and Bobby would spend the holiday at Sam's lake house. B. J.'s plans were unknown. Mike and Scotty had entered to compete in the foot races.

Gramps found a parking place early for the parade. Scotty met Mike later and they lost in the foot race. Mike and his grandparents ate lunch at home, then Gramps took Mike back to the carnival in the afternoon. He met Scotty near the ferris wheel.

Walking through the carnival, they saw Lisa with her mother.

"Want to ride the ferris wheel, Lisa?" Mike asked.

Trish looked at Lisa. "Do you have any money left, Lisa?"

"Not much."

"I'll pay your way," Mike offered.

"What about Scotty?" Lisa asked.

Mike really didn't want Scotty to go with them, but he said it would be all right.

The bar of the seat securely fastened in front of them,

Lisa sat between the two boys. The seats filled, the attendant revved up the motor, and the giant wheel began to ascend. Mike put his arm behind Lisa along the back of the seat. Going over the top, Lisa screamed and fell against Scotty. Mike removed his arm and scooted nearer his side of the seat. He didn't enjoy the rest of the ride.

When the ride was over, he didn't offer to take Lisa or Scotty on anything else.

Lisa rejoined her mother, and Mike and Scotty began walking aimlessly. Mike noticed a man pitching balls at targets in one of the concessions. Suddenly, he heard Scotty say, "That's Dad!"

Having used all the balls allowed, the man turned. Seeing Scotty, his face brightened, and quickly he came over and grabbed Scotty's hand. "Hi, son."

"Dad." Scotty flung himself into his dad's arms, his eyes blurred with tears.

Mike turned his back. He began to walk away, but Scotty reached out and drew Mike forward. Proudly he said, "This is my dad, Mike."

Holding his dad's arm tightly, Scotty asked if they could go and see his mother.

"You think she would let me in?"

"I know she would."

"Let's try then. Where does Mike live?"

Scotty held on to his dad's arm. "He's visiting the Shannons, close to us. You can ride with us, Mike."

"Thanks. I'll stay a while longer. I'm to meet Gramps at six."

Mike wandered among the concessions and side shows. A carnival barker urged him to come in and see the world's fattest lady. Another tried to drum up business for a stage show — a show of the world's most beautiful women. The bingo stand attracted a large crowd, and Mike listened to the man in charge calling out the numbers as he drew them from a box. There were booths giving away kewpie dolls as special prizes. The smell of food — onions, hamburgers, popcorn — permeated the whole area.

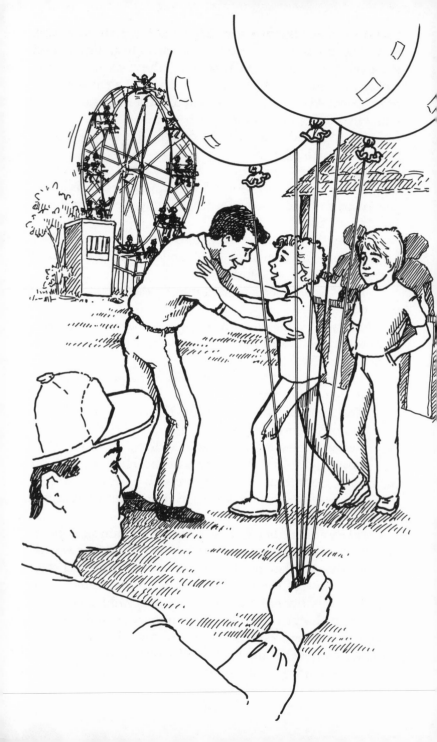

Mike idly watched a vendor winding a mound of pink cotton candy on a stick when someone behind him poked him in the ribs and said, "Hi, again."

It was Lisa, alone this time.

"Oh, hi. Where's Trish?" Mike looked for her mother.

"Sitting on a bench talking to some people she knows."

Lisa didn't ask about Scotty. Mike changed his mind about taking her on another ride. "Want to go on the merry-go-round?"

Lisa smiled. "Sure, why not?"

Hand in hand, they waited in line. When the carousel stopped, they walked to two of the horses, and Mike stood there while Lisa swung herself up onto the back of one of the gaily decorated horses. "These horses are a little small," she laughed.

Sitting on the horse opposite her, again Mike thought of how pretty she was.

The music played, and the horses moved up and down on the metal poles in time with the music as the carousel turned. For Mike, it ended too soon.

"Want to try something else?" he asked as the ride ended.

"I'd like to, but Mom is waiting for me. I'd better go."

"I'll walk with you." Mike took her hand. They threaded their way through the milling crowd.

After Lisa and Trish left, Mike walked to the park and waited there for Gramps. Gran brought a picnic supper. After eating, they lingered at the table and listened to the band concert. Fireworks finished the day.

Making his bed the next morning, Mike heard the doorbell. He called, "I'll get it."

Very excited, Scotty stood there. "Guess what?"

"What?"

"Dad is coming to live with us." Scotty could hardly talk. "I can't stay. Had to tell someone. Dad's home this morning. Have to go back to be with him." He ran off the porch before Mike could say anything.

To himself, Mike muttered, "I hope he stays, Scotty."

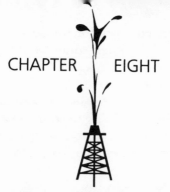

CHAPTER EIGHT

The Campout

Mike entered the kitchen to see Gramps eating another cholesterol-free breakfast. He raised his head and asked, "What's next on your research list?"

Mike began carefully to slice a banana into a cereal bowl. He answered, "The Oil Museum."

"Want to go this morning?"

"I guess."

Gramps spooned the last of the cereal from the bowl and settled back. "Do you remember going to the museum?"

Mike shook his head.

"Your folks were here a couple of years after it opened. You were about three. That's been a while back."

Gramps rose from the table. "Gran said she didn't want to go since she is there every week."

Promptly at 9:00, the doors opened, and Gramps and Mike were the first visitors. Mike looked at displays in the gift cases while Gramps paid the admission.

They walked into the first room. Gramps explained, "These are things from life in the thirties." He pointed to furniture, a Model A roadster, an old gasoline pump.

A wide hall led back into the main area of the museum. To the left of the hall, in an alcove, Mike saw a tall, bronze statue.

"H. L. Hunt." Gramps pointed to the statue. "He

bought many of Dad Joiner's leases. Dad was hard-up for money and had to sell to pay off debts. Mr. Hunt became very wealthy."

Behind leaded glass doors at the end of the hall, Mike saw the main street of a town as it might have been all those years ago. Trucks, two wagons, and a car were stuck in the mud. Four mules hitched to a wagon loaded with furniture were also in the muddy street. They looked so real, Mike reached out to touch them. Then, he leaned over to test the mud. Seeing this, Gramps said simply, "Concrete."

Gramps waved his hand at the stores circling the street. "Everything needed for a small town here, Mike—drug store, newspaper office, post office, barber shop, gas station, general store, machine shop." He pointed to each as he named them.

Oil field tools of all kinds lined a wall inside the gas station. Mike had never seen so many wrenches—Stilson, S, sucker rod, alligator, speed, combination, and others. His eyes roaming over the display, Mike asked, "Did you use all these, Gramps?"

"Yes, Mike, we used them all."

Gramps stopped farther back by two life-sized mannequins dressed in overalls. They were "roughnecks" on an Oilwell Junior Rotary drill rig. "This is the work we did. It was hard and dirty, but there was a good feeling about it."

On a small table, Mike saw a glass-enclosed scale model of a cable tool rig built in 1930, with the derrick made of wood. The little model was complete to the most minute detail.

Moving on up the street, they entered a building with a sign proclaiming "Elevator Ride to the Center of the Earth." The small doors at the back of the room opened like the entrance to a real elevator. Several benches lined a small center aisle. Red curtains covered a puppet stage within the back wall.

Mike and Gramps seated themselves and the ride began.

The red curtains opened, and two eighteen-inch-tall puppets suspended on strings were on the stage. Professor

Rockbottom, the older puppet and a famous geologist, had a long fringe of hair around a bald head, a beard, and a mustache. He was dressed in blue denim overalls. Hank, the boy puppet, wore jeans and moccasins.

The two puppets talked as the elevator supposedly descended through layers of earth. These layers could be seen through a small window in the right wall. Mike mentally repeated the geologic layers: Queen City, Reklaw, Carizzo, Wilcox, Midway, Navarro, Marlbrook, Pecan Gap, Austin Chalk, and Woodbine.

Professor Rockbottom explained that the Austin Chalk above and the Washita below trapped the oil in the Woodbine sand.

"That's where oil was found in the Daisy Bradford Number Three, the Woodbine," Gramps whispered.

Leaving the elevator, Gramps stepped out in the street and asked, "Have you seen enough, Mike?"

"I think so."

"We'd better go and see about Gran."

Mike went swimming with Bobby again that afternoon in Sam's pool. On the way back to Gran's, Mike mentioned Windom's Lake and what a good place it would be to camp.

Bobby shook his head. "They won't let anyone camp there."

"That's where Gramps and I went fishing."

Bobby wasn't convinced. "The whole place is posted."

Mike thought a few minutes. "I didn't see any signs."

"They're on the fence around the pasture."

"We'll ask Gramps."

The house was quiet. Gran had gone somewhere, and Gramps was taking his nap.

The boys slipped back outside, and Bobby went home.

Eating supper later on the patio, Mike asked Gramps again about camping at W BAR W.

Gramps looked at Gran. "What do you think?"

She asked, "How many boys, Mike?"

"Bobby, Sam, B. J., Scotty, and me, if they could all go."

"You'd need an older person along," Gran said, turning

to Gramps.

"Don't look at me." Gramps shook his head. "I'll talk to Jess and help get things together. I'll take the boys out there, but at night I want to be in my own bed."

"Could you call Jess, uh, Mr. Windom, tonight, Gramps?"

"Soon as I finish eating."

Mike thought by listening to the phone conversation that Mr. Windom didn't want them to camp by the lake. When Gramps hung up, Mike asked, "What did he say, Gramps?"

"Same thing Gran said. An older person would have to be along. He would have to know what night — and it's only one night."

A little later, Bobby, Mike, B. J., and Scotty sat around the patio table trying to plan. What older person would go?

Scotty hesitated. "Maybe Dad would go."

"Wanna ask him?" Bobby took charge.

Scotty pushed back his chair and left on the run.

Back in a few minutes, he said, "Dad could go tomorrow since it is Friday. Mom said it would be okay."

Plans were made in a hurry. Bobby made out a list of supplies. Gramps would call Mr. Windom again. Sam should be asked because he had two pop-up tents that would sleep two men each.

The next day was busy. The Rices' white Cadillac pulled into the drive about 3:30. Sam's mother unloaded two tents and an extra bag of snacks for Sam. After Gran told him to wear old sneakers, it surprised Mike to see Sam wearing the new Michael Jordan shoes.

A cool front went through at about 4:00 P.M., lowering the temperature. "More like camping weather," Gramps said.

With everything loaded in Scott's van and Gramps' truck, the campers were on their way. Gramps helped unload his truck and said he'd be back about 10:00 the next day.

Later, set up on the gravel bar, the two pop-up tents looked like blue bubbles. The boys gathered stones and placed them in a circle for a cooking fire. Everything done, a debate ensued about whether to go swimming since it was much cooler. Mr. Scott said the lake water would be warm.

Sam didn't want to swim in lake water. "Too dirty," he said. Bobby elected to follow Sam's wishes. B. J. and Mike would swim for a short while. Scotty stayed close to his dad.

Mike and B. J. splashed and dived in the warm lake water. After one dive, Mike looked toward the camp and saw Sam and Bobby wading in shallow water and pulling the small boat.

The wood brought from town had a nice bed of coals by the time Mike and B. J. dressed after the swim. Mr. Scott said they would have to hunt green sticks to roast the wieners.

The wiener on Sam's stick fell into the fire. He threw the stick down and said, "I didn't want it anyway."

"Come on, Sam. You can have this one." Bobby put he wiener he had roasted between a bun and handed it to Sam.

Sam ate a bite and threw the rest into the fire and went into the tent and brought out the sack of snacks from his mother. He didn't offer the other boys any.

Later, Bobby and Sam sat by the fire. Sam took off the wet Michael Jordan shoes and set them close to the heat. They were covered with mud. Mr. Scott suggested washing the mud off, but Sam answered, "It doesn't matter, Mom will buy me a new pair."

The others roasted marshmallows, and their mouths were covered with black from the crust that formed when the marshmallows caught fire. Fruit and cookies finished the meal.

Dusk fell and swallows swooped low to catch any mosquitoes available. A mockingbird could be heard going through his repertoire of bird calls. Occasionally, a fish flopped in the lake. It was pleasant sitting around the campfire. Darkness descended, and the boys sat there looking into the dancing flames.

Scotty was never far from his dad's side. Mike noticed B. J. looking at Scotty from time to time, but B. J. said nothing.

The moon rose higher in the sky and made a silver reflection on the water, adding to the magic of the night.

"This would be a good time to tell ghost stories," Bobby suggested.

Mike looked at him. "You first, Burton."

Bobby began to talk, making up the story as he went along. He had progressed in the tale to a haunted house, and about that time an owl hooted *"who-o, who-o"* loudly from the woods across the lake. Sam jumped and moved closer to Bobby.

"It's only an owl, Sam." Bobby patted him on the leg.

One story followed another until the fire burned down very low.

Mr. Scott rose and stretched. "Better turn in for the night." He began to scatter dirt on the fire to put it out.

Scotty and his dad had a tent pitched across from the others. They said goodnight and went inside. Sam and Bobby were in one pop-up, and Mike and B. J. in the other.

Mike undressed quickly and unrolled his sleeping bag. Taking a flashlight from the roll, he touched the switch. He saw B. J. sitting on his bedroll, making no effort to get ready for bed.

"What's the matter?" Mike asked.

"Nothing."

"Better get in bed." Mike lay down, turned his back, and waited.

Finally B. J. said, "Turn off the light, Mike."

Tired from all the activity and the swim, Mike fell asleep. He didn't know what time it was, but something woke him. Lying very quietly, he became aware of B. J. crying. He switched on the flashlight.

"Turn off the light!" B. J. hissed.

"What's the matter?" Mike asked for the second time.

"Nothing."

Mike moved over a little closer to B. J.'s bedroll. Putting his hand on B. J.'s shoulder, he said, "Do you want to talk?"

B. J. sniffled and wiped at his eyes. "I hate Scotty."

"Why?"

"Because he can be with his dad."

"Aren't your folks good to you?"

"Yes," B. J. sniffled again, "but it's not the same. I don't know my dad."

Mike didn't know what to say, so he sat there and patted B. J. on the shoulder. B. J. quit crying, and eventually Mike could tell by his breathing that he had fallen asleep.

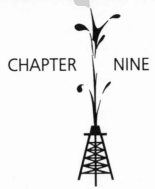

CHAPTER NINE

Guests for Lunch

The boys woke the next morning to the smell of bacon cooking. Mike loved bacon, but never had it smelled or tasted so good as in the open air there by the lake. B. J. looked a little pale and didn't eat much.

Finished with all he could possibly eat, Mike asked, "Could we go swimming again?"

"You need to wait at least thirty minutes," Mr. Scott advised.

"We'd better help Dad clean up," Scotty said as he gathered up paper plates and plastic.

Breakfast things cleared away, Bobby suggested hiking around the lake. Sam put his bare feet into the muddy, wet Michael Jordan shoes. He left them untied.

Walking single-file, they started out with Bobby in the lead. He crossed the dam and led them into the woods on the west. Leaves of past seasons carpeted the ground, and the boys scuffled through them. Blue jays cried *"Thief, thief"* as they approached. Several squirrels scampered up high in trees to safety. Lizards scurried out of the way. Bobby stopped and poked with a stick into a very large ant mound. Dozens of ants swarmed out. The other boys carefully stepped around the ant hill.

Woods to the west and south of the lake were fairly dense, and the hikers covered a lot of ground as Bobby led them back and forth. There was never any doubt he was in charge. He began singing a hiking song, and the others, except Sam, joined in the singing.

The heat of summer had followed yesterday's cool front, and the boys were sweating when they came out of the woods. Sam said he needed to rest. Looking around, Bobby saw a shallow rocky ledge ahead, and he walked toward it. They could sit there and cool off.

Sam ran in front of the others, and in his hurry to get the best seat, he didn't see the coiled spotted body of the snake lying there in the sun. Mr. Scott recognized the rattling sound as the snake shook its tail. Jumping forward, he pulled Sam back out of reach of the forked tongue flipping in and out of the snake's mouth.

Bobby broke into a run, with the others following, and they didn't slow down until back in camp. Out of breath and falling onto the ground, Bobby panted, "What kind of rattlesnake was it?"

"Looked like a diamondback rattler," Mr. Scott calmly answered.

"Boy, Sam is lucky—" Scotty began. He quit speaking at a sign from his dad. Then he noticed how white and shaken Sam looked. In the excitement, Mike forgot about swimming again.

When Gramps came they broke camp, loaded in the camping gear, and went back to Gramps' house. Mr. Scott took Sam home. B. J. and Bobby walked home.

Gran shut off the vacuum cleaner when Mike came into the house. She sat down on a stool and asked, "How was the campout?"

Mike threw his bedroll on the floor. "Gran, that's the neatest place. I hope we can go again."

"Maybe you can. I'm going to the library soon. Do you want to clean up and go with me?"

"I guess."

Mike found a book titled *Oil* on the library shelves. Idly turning the pages, he saw a sketch of a semisubmersible drill rig, the kind of rig used for drilling under water. *Maybe I could make a small model of this for my project,* he thought. He took the book to the circulation desk, and he and Gran checked out.

Leaving the library, they encountered Trish and Lisa coming up the walk. Mike stopped and introduced them to Gran.

Gran held out her hand to Trish and said, "I've heard a lot about you."

Trish grinned. "It was probably bad."

Mike thought maybe Gran could help Lisa and her mother if they got acquainted, so he suggested, "Gran, why don't we go to the Dairy Queen and get Trish and Lisa a Coke and talk?"

Gran turned to Trish and asked, "Do you have time?"

"Let's go, Mom," Lisa urged.

"We have time."

Gran and Trish walked ahead on the way to the nearby Dairy Queen. Mike took Lisa's hand. He overheard Trish replying to Gran's questions.

Sitting in a booth, sipping Cokes, Gran learned that Trish's mother and father were dead. Trish had inherited the house where she and Lisa lived. "That's why we moved here," Trish explained. "The house belonged to me, our trucking business failed, and Bob's health was bad. I had an office job for a while, but the company cut back and those who were hired last were the first to be laid off. My unemployment is about to run out." Trish's shoulders slumped.

Gran asked, "Is Bob home?"

"No, he's still at the VA hospital."

"Why don't you come and have lunch with us?"

Trish hesitated. "We have some shopping to do."

"We can do it later, Mom."

"All right. It's nice of you to ask us, Mrs. Shannon."

Walking back to the library, Lisa and Mike walked slowly and fell behind the other two. So she wouldn't be overheard, Lisa murmured, "You're my best friend, Mike. The best friend I have here."

"What about Scotty?"

"I wanted to tease you. Scotty is a friend, too, but not my best friend."

That settled one problem.

Gramps said hello but didn't say anything else when Trish walked into the house. He looked closely at Lisa, as though he wanted to see if she had any bruises.

Trish offered to help, and Gran put her to work slicing vegetables for the salad. Lisa and Mike set the patio table.

Trish ate some of the salad, and finally she put the fork on the table and leaned back in her chair. She turned toward Gramps. "Mr. Shannon, I'm sorry to have been so rude when you were at our house."

Embarrassed, Gramps said, "That's all right."

Her eyes on the iced tea glass, Trish turned it slowly. "It's been so long since we've had any friends that we've forgotten manners. I think it is important for Lisa to be with others her age." They waited for her to continue. "The way things are, I don't know how to work it out."

Gran offered, "Maybe we could help. We could be adopted parents or something like that — take the place of the family you have lost."

Trish looked at Gran with tears in her eyes. "Thanks, Mrs. Shannon. I haven't had anyone to turn to since Ron and Mama died."

Gran rose from the table. "That's settled."

By the time Trish and Lisa left, it was arranged. Trish still had a phone, and they would keep in touch.

Skeptical of any relationship with Bob, Gramps brought up the subject during supper. Eating the last bite on his plate, he leaned back in his chair. "I guess Trish is all right, but I can't think of ever having anything to do with Bob."

"You don't think he can be helped?" Gran asked.

"Maybe so and maybe not. He's got a long way to go."

All Gran said was, "We'll see."

CHAPTER TEN

Learning More

Mike lay in bed the next morning, thinking about the semisubmersible rig. He picked up the book containing the picture of the rig and tried to imagine how difficult it would be to build. Looking at his research list, he saw that two items remained.

Gran tapped on the door and called out, "Breakfast, Mike."

Gramps' plate contained scrambled eggs. He pointed to them with his fork and said, "Good breakfast."

Mike seated himself and Gran placed a plate of scrambled eggs and toast in front of him. After taking a few bites, he said, "Gramps, saltwater disposal and pump jacks are on the research list."

"I know. I thought we'd go and see both this morning if Gran doesn't need help."

Gran told them to go ahead. She would do a few house chores and then drive out to Trish's for a few minutes. "I'll call her first to see if it's all right."

Mike hated to miss seeing Lisa, but he needed to finish his research.

Later, seated in the car, Gramps said, "We can see pump jacks and Christmas trees in many places, but there are some new installations near town."

"What's the difference between pump jacks and Christmas trees?" Mike asked.

"Christmas trees contain a series of valves to regulate the flow from free-flowing wells."

"They're artificial trees, huh, Gramps?"

Gramps smiled. "You could say that. Pump jacks are used in wells that are not free-flowing."

A short distance from the business area of town the highway divided to form a "Y." On the right side of the curve, Gramps pulled into an open space. Before them Mike saw one of the pump jacks, and to him it looked like a huge metal grasshopper.

Leaving the car, Mike could hear the machinery clanking as the metal head slowly moved up and down.

"Do you think you might want to make one of these for your project?" Gramps asked.

Mike walked closer. The long metal beam with the head was supported on a metal derrick. Gramps began to explain how it worked.

"This is actually a mechanical pump connection that raises the oil artificially when it no longer flows of its own pressure."

"Does it work like a water pump, Gramps?"

"It's a simple suction pump with a moving piston, an inlet valve at the bottom of the pump cylinder, and a discharge valve at the top of the piston."

"How big is the pump?"

"Usually one and a half to three and a half inches in diameter. It operates with strokes forty-two to eighty-six inches long and at a speed of ten to twenty strokes per minute."

"Let's time the strokes," Mike suggested.

Gramps took out his pocketwatch. "You count the strokes, Mike. I'll watch the minute hand."

Mike had counted ten strokes when Gramps called time. The iron contraption was clanking all the time, and an ooze of heavy black oil coated the rod going into the well.

"See, Mike, the pump is lowered to a point near the bottom of the well and linked to a seesaw arrangement or beam at the surface by steel rods." Gramps pointed to a metal housing. "The motor is in here, and it drives a band wheel by a belt." He pointed to each thing as he talked. "The rotation of the huge half wheels turns a crank. This produces the up and down motion of the beam."

Gramps pointed to a large pipe running from the pump several hundred yards to a storage tank, most of the pipe underground. "The oil is going into that tank."

Gramps led Mike a little farther on to a large, newly cleared area where a Christmas tree was in operation. "There's not much to explain here. The valves can be adjusted to control the flow of oil. It goes back there into one of those two storage tanks."

Mike saw three huge tanks several yards from the Christmas tree. "What's the other tank for, Gramps?"

"Water. One for water, two for oil."

Gramps started back to the car. "Let's go see the salt-water pits."

It was some distance to one of the pits off in an area by itself. Mike could see a thick black layer of oil on top of the water in the pit.

"Mike, if I remember the figures right, there was about four hundred thousand barrels of salt water per day coming to the surface in the East Texas Oil Field around 1941."

"That's a lot of water. What did they do with all of it?"

"First, do you know why the water had salt in it?"

Mike thought a minute. "If it came up with the oil, the salt would have been sea water trapped in the oil pockets when water covered the land."

"Right—trapped many millions of years ago. You know oil rises to the top of water and gas will rise above the oil. But to get back to your question. In the early days, they tried several ways to get rid of the salt water—put it in pits, released it into rivers and streams, and even tried evaporation."

"Gramps, the salt would kill fish, wouldn't it?"

"Yes, not only fish but about everything it touched. So something had to be done. The open system of disposal was chosen as the best way then. They aerated the salt water—

mixed it with air — to oxidize the iron. Chlorine was added to kill bacteria and algae. Alum and lime were added, and time allowed for sedimentation. After this, the treated water was injected into abandoned wells so it could reenter the Woodbine sand and help maintain pressure. That was the way of treatment in the fifties."

"Has it changed, Gramps?"

"Quite a lot."

"How?"

"Now there is a flow line from the wells, and the oil and water go into huge separator tanks six to eight feet in diameter and fifteen feet high."

"What happens in the tank, Gramps?"

"A fire tube, burning gas that is controlled by an automatic thermostat, heats the liquid to a certain temperature. This causes the water and oil to separate. The water then runs into a pit or it might go through several pits and then by pipe back into the wells. The men who work for Saltwater Disposal Company check the instruments for controlling things several times a day. This prevents problems."

Gramps was silent for a while. "I'm about talked out, Mike. Let's go home."

"Okay. Thanks, Gramps."

Arriving at the house, Mike went to his room and added all he remembered to his notes.

Gramps stuck his head in the door. "There's a note on the kitchen table for you."

In Gran's handwriting the note read, "Scotty called and wants you to go swimming. I'll be back by noon."

Mike called Scotty, and they decided to go to the pool about 1:00. Mike and Gramps fixed some sandwiches and made an extra plate for Gran. Mike wished she would come home so he could find out about Lisa.

Gran came out on the patio as Mike took the last bite of his sandwich. With his mouth full, he asked, "How's Lisa?"

Gran laughed. "Why didn't you ask me about Trish?"

Swallowing quickly, Mike asked, "How is Trish?"

"Lisa is fine and so is her mother. Trish found an ad in

last night's Help Wanted section in the paper. The college needs a secretary in one of the departments. She had a resume all ready and will take it in this afternoon."

Gramps had pulled out a chair for Gran and stood there waiting for her to be seated. "I hope she gets the job and gets rid of Bob." Gramps wasn't going to change his feelings about Bob.

Mike and Scotty swam until time for Scotty to run his paper route. Mike offered to go with him for two reasons — the main one being it would give him a chance to see Lisa.

Lisa's house was one of the last on the route. Not seeing anyone, Mike asked Scotty to ride around to the back with him.

"The truck is gone. They must still be in town," Mike said almost to himself.

Mike and Gramps watched a Ranger ballgame until 11:00. The game started late and went into extra innings.

Gramps yawned on the way to bed and remarked, "I'm getting too old for this."

In the middle of a dream about camping, Mike became aware of the doorbell ringing. Not fully awake, he lay in bed listening. Someone pounded on the front door. He heard Gramps muttering in the hall.

Mike jumped from bed and followed Gramps to the door. Switching on the porch light, Gramps opened the door.

Bobby stood there, white-faced and trembling.

Gramps opened the storm door and pulled Bobby into the living room. "What's the matter, son?" he asked.

"Someone tried to break into the house." Bobby had difficulty in speaking.

Gran came into the room, pulling on a robe. Hearing Bobby's words, she asked, "Where are your folks?"

Bobby began to sob. "I don't know."

Gran turned on a lamp and led Bobby to a chair. "Sit down, Bobby. Tell us what happened."

Bobby rubbed his fists across his eyes. "I watched a late show on TV and decided to go to bed. I couldn't sleep, and it wasn't long before I heard a noise. Lady jumped off the bed and started barking."

Seeing he was very upset, Gran said, "Take your time, Bobby."

"Well, I opened the bedroom door and Lady ran to the kitchen. I followed her and could see someone trying to get the door open."

"Do you have a yard light?" Gramps asked.

"No. McDougals had their light on, and I could see by that." Bobby shuddered at recalling the incident.

"Take it easy, Bobby. You're all right now." Mike moved to the floor by Bobby's chair.

Gramps started toward the phone. "We'd better call the police."

The call completed, Gramps suggested going out on the porch to watch for the police car. He realized he and Mike were in pajamas, so they put on robes. Mike noticed Bobby always managed to stay behind Gramps.

In a few minutes car lights could be seen coming up the street. Gramps walked out to the curb. The white car stopped. Two officers were in the car. The black patrolman driving introduced himself as Bill Butler and his companion as John Dwyer. Introducing himself, Gramps explained he had been the one who called.

"Where is the house?" Butler asked.

"Up five houses on the other side of the street." A street light provided enough illumination for Gramps to point.

"Is anyone at the house?" the officer questioned.

"No. Bobby," Gramps said, pulling him forward, "was there alone at the time."

Officer Dwyer came around to where Gramps and the boys were standing. "I'll walk up there with them, Bill," he said.

Arriving at the house, they heard Lady barking. Bobby took them to the front door and inside, and Mike felt proud of the way Bobby explained what had happened. He led the way to the kitchen door, and upon examination, the policemen found where the screen had been pulled loose on the outside and the storm door unlocked.

Dwyer pointed to scratch marks on the inside of the kitchen door. "Were those on there before?" he asked.

"I don't think so. Dad painted it not very long ago."

Officer Dwyer looked at Lady. "The dog probably frightened them away."

Lady stood silently near Bobby. He hugged her around the neck and patted her head and said, "Good girl."

The policemen searched the backyard with a high-powered flashlight. Evidently, the prowler had crawled over the chain link fence.

Returning to the house, Patrolman Dwyer turned to Bobby. "Do you have some place to spend the rest of the night?"

Before Bobby could answer, Gramps spoke up. "Yes, he has. He can stay with us."

Mike looked at Bobby's pajamas. "You're already dressed for bed. You can come as you are."

Bobby grinned weakly.

Back outside, they saw a car coming up the street. It was Bobby's mother and dad. His dad stopped quickly, jumped from the car, and raced over to Bobby. "What's wrong, son?"

In a disgusted tone, Policeman Butler said, "Someone tried to break in the house. Apparently the dog frightened them off."

Mrs. Burton got out of the car, stumbled, ran to Bobby and threw her arms around him. "Oh, baby, did they hurt you?"

Mike could smell alcohol strongly.

Bobby managed to wiggle away from his mother. "I'm all right."

Gramps and Mike walked back home. Once inside the house, Mike could see the fury on Gramps' face. He sat in a chair without saying anything for a few minutes. "What in the world is the matter with those people? Leaving that boy alone until all hours of the night, not knowing where they are, and at the mercy of anybody or anything that might come along. And to add insult to injury, coming home drunk at, what time is it anyway?" He was so angry he fairly sputtered.

Gran quietly said, "It's two o'clock."

Gramps shook his head. "I'd like to give them a piece of my mind."

That was exactly what Gran did later in the morning, when Mrs. Burton came to apologize. Gran told her in no uncertain terms what she thought.

Mike heard Mrs. Burton weakly try to explain, "But Bobby is so mature—"

Gran interrupted, "How old is Bobby?"

"He's eleven—soon twelve."

"He's not mature. Not mature enough to be left alone until all hours of the night and not knowing where his parents are." Gran didn't mince words.

"Oh, you're old-fashioned, Mrs. Shannon. Kids nowadays learn early to look out for themselves. They grow up quicker."

Gran said nothing more, knowing it was probably useless. She rose and stood by the front door silently until Bobby's mother left.

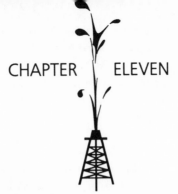

CHAPTER ELEVEN

A Dance with Lisa

After the incident with the prowler, things quieted down in the neighborhood. Gramps talked with Charles Butterworth and learned the police had a suspect in some other burglaries but needed more evidence.

Trish called Gran and reported she was scheduled for an interview with the personnel director at the local college. Very excited, she called back later to tell Gran she had been hired. It would be a month before she started to work — about the time Lisa's fall term began.

Hearing Trish's news, Gramps asked, "Is Bob still at the VA hospital?"

"I guess so," Gran replied.

"I hope he doesn't foul this up for Trish."

Gran made no reply.

Mike mowed the yard in the afternoon. He didn't see Scotty deliver their paper, but about 6:00 P.M. Scotty rang the doorbell. His head still wet from the shower, Mike came to the door drying his hair.

Scotty stepped inside and gave Mike a small, white envelope. Turning it over, Mike asked, "What's this?"

"Invitation to my birthday party."

Opening the envelope, Mike read that it was Scotty's twelfth birthday. The time for the party would be Friday from 7:00 to 9:30.

"Dad will take us to the miniature golf course on Darnley Road." Scotty's eyes shone at the mention of his dad.

"Who else is coming?" Mike asked.

"My cousin, Jene, is coming, and Mom thought we should ask some other girls so Jene won't be the only girl."

"Could you ask Lisa?"

"I took her invitation on the route with me."

"Good."

Scotty grinned. "I knew that would please you."

Later, Mike shopped for a present and chose a striped knit shirt. Gran said they needed wrapping paper and a card. Mike found a funny card with Garfield on the front.

Mike helped Gramps around the place the next day. Late in the afternoon they went fishing, but the fish were too small to keep.

Scotty waited in his yard Friday evening to welcome his guests. He introduced Mike, Bobby, and Sam to the four girls sitting on the front steps. Mike briefly noticed each one.

Scotty's cousin Jene had long, almost black hair and the biggest black eyes Mike had ever seen. Another girl, Lynn Stewart, jumped from the step and came toward the boys when Scotty mentioned her name. Her blond hair, cut short on the sides and back, lay plastered on her forehead — a forehead beaded with sweat — in long bangs. She pushed the bangs nervously to one side.

Painfully thin, Stacy McInnis seemed shy and ill at ease when Scotty mentioned her name. Her family had recently moved three doors down from the Scotts.

Mike didn't hear Brandi's last name because he saw Lisa getting out of her mother's car, and he walked over to meet her.

Scotty told them Lisa's name, and again Mike thought of how pretty she looked.

Scotty's mom and dad came from the house. His mother asked, "Did you introduce the girls, Scotty?"

"Yes, ma'am."

Mr. Scott moved toward the van. "Let's load up." Then he asked, "Is everyone here?"

Looking around, Scotty said, "Everyone but B. J."

Mike stepped out to the curb and looked down the street. B. J. slowly walked along. "Hurry up, man!" Mike called. B. J. didn't walk much faster, but Mike waited for him. He kept glancing at the others loading into the van and hoped Lisa would save a seat for him. She saved a seat, and everyone tried to talk at once on the way to the golf course.

A large sign about two miles from town advertised "DARNLEY AMUSEMENT PARK." A red arrow pointed to a narrow, black-topped road.

A short distance down the blacktop, Mr. Scott pulled the van into a parking lot. He said, "You all wait here." Turning to Mrs. Scott, he said, "Let's go inside."

The long, dark red building had a sign across the front indicating it was the clubhouse.

Mr. Scott and the owner soon returned. Everyone tumbled from the van. The owner gave each person a golf club and golf ball. "Do you know how to play?" he asked.

Most of the group had played before, but he explained they should go in groups of four instead of waiting for all to have a turn on each of the eighteen putting greens.

Jene pushed Scotty forward. "You go first because it's your birthday."

"No, I'll be last," Scotty said, stepping to the end of the line.

On several of the greens Sam didn't get his ball in the hole in the allowed five shots. Finally, Mike saw him throw his club on the ground, and he said he didn't want to play any longer.

Mike picked up the club, gave it to Sam, and said, "You can do better than that, Sam. Don't spoil Scotty's birthday."

Play proceeded fairly well after that. B. J. and Scotty had the lowest scores when everyone had finished.

The group proceeded to the clubhouse. Mrs. Scott was waiting on the porch to direct them into the large room. The room, decorated like an old-time soda fountain, had soft lights illuminating wire ice cream tables and chairs placed at intervals. For this occasion, bunches of balloons swayed gently in the breeze of an overhead fan. A girl in a red and white candy-striped short skirt and blouse waited by the soda fountain to serve them.

With a great amount of scraping of chairs, everyone found a seat. Mrs. Scott brought a large, decorated sheet cake over to where Scotty sat. She lighted the twelve candles and told Scotty to make a wish. He blew out all the candles with one try. The serving girl brought out plates of ice cream to go with the cake.

Scotty opened his presents. Most of the guests gave him money, and this surprised Mike because it wasn't customary in West Texas.

Dancing followed the refreshments. A small side room had a dance floor and record player. The owner of the park asked what music they liked. Lisa said she could slow dance, so Mike suggested that. He held out his hand to Lisa and said, "Want to try?"

"Mike, I'm really not a very good dancer."

"You'll do all right."

Mike placed his arm lightly around her waist. As long as he kept his distance, they did fairly well. Lisa was wearing sandals, and Mike concentrated on the steps so he wouldn't step on her feet. He had danced some before, but never with a girl he liked as much as Lisa.

Mike didn't ask anyone else to dance, even though Jene and Lynn looked at him invitingly. Mr. and Mrs. Scott danced together several times. The other boys had a tendency to stand by themselves along one side of the room. Finally, Stacy and Brandi went onto the floor together, and they more or less swayed in time to the music. Lynn and Jene followed them and danced. Lisa stayed by Mike's side.

At 9:30 Mr. Scott moved toward the door, and Scotty soon followed with the others falling in line for the ride back to Scotty's house.

Mike and Lisa walked to Gran's. Trish was waiting there and asked Lisa if she had a good time.

Looking at Mike, Lisa said, "It was super, Mom."

CHAPTER TWELVE

Bob Is Back

On the Saturday after the party, Mike and Scotty went swimming. Jene, still visiting the Scotts, went with them. Scotty's mother picked them up at about 3:30 so Scotty could run his route.

Being with Jene made Mike think of Lisa. Before leaving Scott's house, he turned to Scotty and asked, "Could I use the blue bike for a while?"

"Sure. Do you want to go on the route with me?"

"No. I thought I'd ride out to Lisa's."

"Oh." Scotty gave him a knowing look.

Mike took his wet suit home and told Gramps he would be back later.

Lisa was home and so was Bob. Standing on the back porch, he looked up as Mike rode around the back corner of the house. Mike braked quickly and waited. Bob didn't say anything. He turned and walked into the house.

Mike didn't know what to do. He glanced toward one of the windows and saw Lisa looking out. She motioned for him to go around to the front. Joining him there a few minutes later, they slowly walked down the driveway.

Pushing the bike, Mike looked at Lisa. His concern for her was noticeable. "Are you all right?"

"Yes. Mom says Bob is better. He still isn't anything like Daddy, but I guess that time is over." She walked on slowly. "If he doesn't get mean, maybe things will work out."

"I hope so, Lisa. Gran wants to help you and Trish, but Gramps doesn't like Bob."

Lisa smiled slightly. "Neither does anyone else."

"I'd better go. Will you call us if you need help?"

"Yes, Mike. It's good to have you for a friend."

His heart in his eyes as he looked at her, Mike said, "More than a friend, Lisa."

He rode a short distance and looked back. She was still standing there. She waved and turned toward the house.

Mike worried all the way to Gran's. He burst into the house, calling in a loud voice, "Gran!"

Gran came in from the patio. "What's the matter?"

"Bob's back home."

"How did he act?" Before Mike could answer, she asked another question. "How do you know he's back?"

"I rode out there. He didn't say anything. When he saw me, he went back in the house."

"Are Lisa and Trish all right?"

"Lisa is, but I didn't see Trish."

Listening to the conversation, Gramps' lips compressed in a hard, thin line.

Mike took Scotty's bike home but didn't see anyone. He watched TV that evening with Gramps and Gran, but there was little conversation. At bedtime, Gran said, "I'll call Trish or see her tomorrow."

Mike felt relieved — to a degree.

Mike and Gran went to church the next morning, and Gran decided to drive by Trish's house before going home. She drove around to the back of the house. Trish heard the car and came out, glancing nervously toward the back door. Lisa followed her mother.

"Is everything all right, Trish?" Gran asked.

"Sometimes I have hope, Mrs. Shannon. Other times, I don't know."

Bob opened the back door and stood there looking in their direction. Unshaved, he still didn't look as bad as the first time Mike had seen him.

Gran said very quietly, "I guess we had better go. Our home is open to you and Lisa if you need a place to stay."

"Thanks, Mrs. Shannon."

Going down the drive, Mike turned in the seat and saw Lisa standing there alone.

Gran didn't know at the time how soon she would have to make good on her offer.

CHAPTER THIRTEEN

The Daisy Bradford #3

Monday morning during breakfast, Gran said, "I can't get Trish and Lisa out of my mind. I hope nothing is wrong out there."

"Call her and find out," Gramps suggested.

After the call, Gran reported everything seemed to be all right. Trish told her Bob was trying to control his drinking.

"I wouldn't bet any money he'd quit," Gramps grumbled.

Mike knew there wasn't much more time to get his research notes together. He worked on the notes for some time, but needed to make a sketch of the pump jack. Gramps took him back to the location of the pump jack and sat there while Mike sketched it.

Mike and Gramps worked in the yard in the afternoon. After supper, Mike wandered outside. The street ended just past Bobby's house, and someone had put up a basketball hoop and backboard on the grass there. Mike couldn't believe what he saw. Bobby and his dad were shooting baskets!

Seeing Mike, Bobby yelled, "Come on, Mike, and take some shots!"

Holding the ball, Mr. Burton stopped and waited as Mike approached. He stepped forward and grasped Mike's hand. "I want to thank you and your grandparents for help-

ing Bobby the other night. I guess my wife and I needed something drastic to happen to wake us up."

Embarrassed, Mike said, "It wasn't any trouble."

Telling Gran about it later, she laughed and shook her head. "Will wonders never cease. I didn't think anything would change those people."

The next day, Gramps and Mike started to go to the grocery store for Gran. Mike noticed Gramps headed in the opposite direction. He said, "Hey, Gramps, this isn't the way to the store."

Gramps didn't volunteer much information. "Want to show you something."

Gramps drove south from town. Signs all along the highway had the name of a particular lease on them. Narrow oiled roads led into the leases. Pumps and storage tanks could be seen, along with the names of major oil companies such as Mobil and Exxon.

An East Texas Oil Production Field Office had the name of Placid Oil Company on it. "Isn't Placid the name of the company that gave the money for the East Texas Oil Museum?" Mike asked.

"Yes, Mike. Mr. Hunt's daughter is an owner of Placid."

Gramps turned off the highway into a little roadside park. The historical marker stated this was the site of the Daisy Bradford #3. Getting out of the car, Mike read the sign. In part, it read:

> The equipment consisted of an old rotary rig powered by a single cylinder engine, one 45 HP boiler and one old cotton gin boiler fired with soggy oak and pine chunks by a roustabout. On Sept. 5, 1930 the drill stem logged at 3536' into the Woodbine formation showed oil. A better rig was brought in and on Oct. 3, 1930 the well blew in and oil went over the crown block. In the first 30 years 3½ billion barrels of oil was produced.

"This is how it happened, Mike. Can you imagine what this meant? There were no jobs — the Depression had gripped the country. And then all at once, Dad Joiner struck oil. This started the East Texas Oil Boom." Gramps sat there, lost in memory of those days so long ago.

He talked more on the way to the store. "People don't realize how long oil has been in use. Many, many years ago oil and water were forced to the surface by changes in the earth's crust. The water evaporated and left behind a heavy, oily substance called bitumen. Noah coated the Ark with bitumen."

"Noah?"

"Yes, Noah. Indians in Brazil tipped arrows with bitumen. They lit the tips and fired them at their enemies." Gramps quit talking to pass a slow moving truck.

"The Chinese piped oil through bamboo and used it to burn in lamps at the time of Julius Caesar." Arriving at the store, Gramps concluded, "It's been around for a long time."

Gramps paused and sat back for a minute before getting from the truck. "There is one other thing. You can be proud as a Texan because the discovery of the East Texas Oil Field helped the United States and their Allies to win World War II."

"Dad Joiner's lack of money turned out pretty good then, huh, Gramps?"

"You could say that."

CHAPTER FOURTEEN

The Fire

The next day Gran told them she needed some cosmetics from the drug store. After she left, Gramps and Mike went outside, and Gramps left the patio door open in case the phone rang. He and Mike were sitting quietly in the glider, watching two squirrels at play. They were amazed at the distance the squirrels could leap from one branch to another.

Suddenly, Gran burst through the open patio door and exclaimed, "I knew it!"

Seeing how upset she was, Gramps rose, pulled out a chair, and said, "Sit down a minute." Then, "Knew what?"

"Bob is acting up. Trish was in the drug store and said he started on drugs again because his leg hurt."

Instantly, Mike became concerned. "I hope he doesn't hurt Lisa."

"I told Trish she could come here if he got mean."

Gramps thought it over. "That's about all we can do. It's up to Trish to make the decisions."

Gran said she would stay near the phone in case Trish called.

Mike wandered out on the street that afternoon. He didn't know what to think. He could go on the route with Scotty and try to see Lisa. But Gramps said Trish should make the decisions, so Mike decided to wait.

Around 10:00 that evening, Gramps tuned into the evening news. Gran seemed nervous. She went to the door and looked out at the street several times.

The news over, they said goodnight and went to their rooms. Gran came into Mike's room later and sat down on the bed. She said, "Mike, I am really worried about Trish and Lisa. We'll go out there in the morning."

Lying awake in bed, Mike heard the long, drawn out wail of a siren twice. It only added to his apprehension.

About midnight, the doorbell rang. Gramps turned on the porch light and opened the door. Trish and Lisa stood there. Smudges of black were on their faces and clothes. Lisa's eyes were wide with fright. Trembling violently, Trish began to cry.

Gramps helped them inside the house and had them sit down. Sensing something very wrong, Gran came out of her room. Seeing Trish and Lisa, she hugged them and sat on the arm of the chair where Trish was sitting. She kept patting Trish on the shoulder. Finally, she said, "Now, tell us what happened."

"We had a fire, a terrible fire." Wiping her nose and trying to control her sobs, Trish began to talk, hesitantly at first. "I hoped Bob would try to do better, but he began drinking yesterday afternoon. Lisa and I went to the seven o'clock movie to get away." As though surprised, she said, "I don't remember the movie."

Reliving it, Trish began to sob again. Gran kept shaking her head, and her face mirrored the pity she felt.

Presently, quiet again, Trish resumed her story. "I could see the flames before we came close to the house — flames shooting upward through the roof."

"No one else had seen the fire?" Gran questioned.

"Apparently not. Lisa and I jumped from the truck and ran around to the back. Through the window we could see the fire inside. Somehow we managed to get the back door open and found Bob lying there on the floor. I thought he was dead." She shuddered.

Lisa sat there speechless. Mike moved closer and sat on

the floor next to her. Her voice barely audible, Trish continued, "The flames were so hot I don't know how we managed, but we pulled him outside. I felt his pulse and he moved slightly once we got him in the fresh air."

"Where is Bob now?" Gramps asked.

"In the hospital. Some man stopped. I don't know his name. He sent an ambulance and the firetruck."

This explained the sirens Mike heard.

"I'll fix some cold drinks." Gran rose and headed for the kitchen. "Oh, Trish, would you and Lisa like to wash off the black? There are two of my robes in the bathroom you can put on for now."

Trish rose unsteadily to her feet. "Come on, Lisa, maybe we will feel better." Lisa followed her into the bathroom.

Gran called after them. "There is some good lotion and dusting powder on the vanity. Help yourselves."

Lisa and Trish reappeared later wearing the robes and looking refreshed and calmer.

Settled with large glasses filled with Coke and ice, Gran asked, "Was Bob badly burned?"

"No, not really. I guess it is a miracle. The doctor thought he suffered mostly from smoke inhalation. Being on the floor probably saved him, but I don't think he would have survived much longer." Gran couldn't tell whether Trish was sorry or glad.

"You are both worn out. Let's get some sleep, and when it gets light, we can make some plans. Trish, you and Lisa can sleep in the spare bedroom. It has clean sheets on the bed already, waiting for someone to use them."

Sitting on the side of the bed, Trish looked up at Gran, and her eyes again filled with tears. "Mrs. Shannon, now we've lost everything."

"It's not that bad. You and Lisa are alive, and we'll work out something." She again hugged Trish and Lisa. "Get some rest."

Mike waited in the hall for Gran. Seeing his anxiety, she said, "They will be fine, Mike. Don't worry."

Mike knew they could depend on Gran to help.

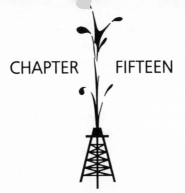

CHAPTER FIFTEEN

A Place for Trish and Lisa

Wan and tired, Trish and Lisa appeared at the breakfast table wearing Gran's robes. Both showed signs of the terrible strain of the previous night.

Bustling around in her usual cheerful manner, Gran smiled and said, "We are so glad to have you here, and we will help you all we can."

Trish fingered a piece of toast. "I don't know where to turn. My job doesn't start for several weeks. We have no place to stay and no money. I have another unemployment check coming, and that is it."

Gran looked at Gramps, and he nodded. "We can offer one solution. Gramps and I have money we keep in reserve for times such as this. Gramps will put enough in the bank this morning in your name to tide you over this bad time."

"I can't take it, Mrs. Shannon. I don't—"

Gran put her fingers over Trish's lips. "*Sh-sh.* It isn't a loan. It is a gift and there is no obligation. You see, Trish, one time long ago we were helped, and this is our way of repaying that kindness."

Choked with emotion, all Trish could say was, "Thanks."

Returning from the bank, Gramps said he would weed the flower borders. "Need a little outside activity," he explained.

Wearing some clothes of Gran's, Lisa and Trish accompanied by Gran went to town to shop.

Mike helped Gramps with the weeding. All the time he worked, he tried to think of some way he might help Lisa and Trish.

Coming from town with their arms full of packages, Lisa couldn't wait to model the new clothes. Later, wearing new outfits, Trish and Lisa left for the hospital to visit Bob. After they left, Gramps turned to Mike, his eyes twinkling. "Always remember, Mike, there is nothing like a shopping trip to make a woman, young or old, feel better."

"Lisa is pretty, don't you think so, Gramps?"

"Oh, so that's the way it is." Gramps chuckled. "Almost as pretty as Gran."

Mike sat on the curb waiting for Trish and Lisa. He saw Scotty coming up the street delivering papers. Scotty rode over to the curb and stopped.

"Mike, did you know Lisa's house burned?"

"Yes, she and her mother are staying here."

"What are they going to do?"

"I don't know, Scotty. They need a place to live."

Scotty sat on the bike for a few minutes thinking.

"Mike, do you remember going on the route with me and delivering papers to apartments near the college?"

"Yes," Mike nodded. "You said there were so many your arm got tired. What about it?"

"A man there canceled his paper yesterday and moved out. If you want to go with me now, maybe you could find out about it."

"I'll tell Gramps."

Riding the blue bike, Mike pedaled along the route with Scotty. The U-shaped, one-story apartment complex surrounded a central garden area. Scotty pointed, "That's it, number nineteen."

Mike parked the bike and walked up to ring the bell. The venetian blinds were closed, and no one came to the door. He turned toward Scotty and said, "No one here."

Scotty pointed out the office. "Ask there. I'd better go on, Mike. See you later."

"Thanks, Scotty. I'll leave the bike at your house."

Mike opened the door at the office, and a buzzer alerted a heavy blond in a tight pink blouse. She turned off the TV and stepped up to the counter. In a high-pitched voice, she inquired, "May I help you?"

Mike assumed his most adult manner. "Could you tell me if there is an empty apartment?"

Peering at him through gold-rimmed glasses, the woman looked him over from head to foot. "For who?"

"A friend and her mother."

Wondering if she could believe him, she asked, "What's their name?"

"Trish and Lisa Jacobs." Mike forgot Bob.

"Is she adult?"

"Trish is. She is Lisa's mother."

"There is a vacancy. But it won't be vacant long, you can bet. If she is interested, tell her to see me pronto." The girl turned back to the TV.

"Yes, ma'am. I'll tell her." He turned and almost ran to the door and then stopped. "Pardon me, ma'am, will you not rent it until she comes?"

"If she hurries."

So excited about the possibility of helping Lisa, Mike rode back to Gran's as fast as he could pedal. Seeing Lisa's truck in the driveway, he jumped off the bike and burst into the house. Panting from all the effort, he could hardly speak.

"Lisa, Trish, I've found an empty apartment."

Stopping to catch his breath, Mike told them the details. He said that they must hurry before someone else rented the place.

Furnished, the apartment would be satisfactory. It had been redecorated recently, and cleaning had been done that day. The manager said they were lucky because the "For Rent" ad would have been in the paper the next day.

Mike and Lisa walked to Scotty's later with the bike. Leaving the bike in the garage, Mike took her hand on the way to Gran's.

Squeezing his fingers, Lisa said, "Thanks, Mike, for finding the apartment. It will be a lot better living there."

Mike wanted to take all the credit, and he didn't answer for a few minutes. He had to be honest, so he said, "Scotty told me about the place."

"Yes, but you were the one who worked it all out."

CHAPTER SIXTEEN

Nothing Left

Early the next morning, Trish said, "Lisa and I should go ahead and get settled in the apartment. There isn't much to move, but we'll need groceries and other supplies. First, I would like to go out to the house and see if there is anything left."

Gran wiped off the table. "Let me finish, Trish, and I'll go with you."

Gramps overheard the conversation. "Let Mike go on with Trish and Lisa. You can ride out later with me, Gran."

Arriving at the house, Trish drove the truck slowly up the drive. Nothing of the house remained but a burned-out shell. Mike sensed what a bad experience the fire had been when he saw the blackened ruin. Glancing quickly at Trish, he noticed her chin trembling and her hands shaking on the steering wheel. Lisa sat white-faced and silent.

Trish parked the truck, and they started toward the charred remains. It was weird—the icebox, stove, and other appliances stood blackened and damaged beyond repair. The solitary brick chimney towered over all like a sentinel. Mike noticed the scorched leaves and branches of the trees surrounding the house.

Sadly, Trish remarked, "We had little happiness here, but it was our home."

Picking up an unburned heavy stick, Trish began poking around in the blackened mass. She shook her head. "It's no use. There is nothing left here." She turned and started back to the truck. Mike and Lisa followed.

Trish started to turn the truck around when Gramps and Gran arrived. Gramps hopped down and called out, "Leaving so soon?"

Slowing the truck, Trish answered, "There is nothing here, Mr. Shannon."

Gramps turned to Gran. "Why don't you go with Trish? Mike and I will look around a little."

They drove off without Trish looking back.

Gramps talked to himself as he walked around the remains of the house. "No use in poking around in there. Nothing left."

His inspection of the house finished, Gramps stopped in the backyard. "You know, Mike, I remember working on a drill rig somewhere back there." He pointed west behind the house. "Quite a ways back there, I think." He kept trying to remember. "The drilling company I worked for drilled that well for Exxon and I think the well came in. Course, that was a long time ago."

Mike tried to follow Gramps' thoughts. What would the well have to do with Trish's house burning?

Gramps began to walk. "Let's go back there and see."

A fence overgrown and impenetrable with vines of some kind bordered the back of the yard, making it impossible to see much. Gramps pulled on the vines and made a place big enough to squeeze through. The old fence was so rusted and rotten it didn't present a problem. A pasture at one time, now the land showed the neglect of years.

Gramps kept walking toward the west, Mike silent by his side. After a time, they topped a slight rise. There in the distance they could see an old pump jack, rusted and standing alone in the field.

Mike could hear the excitement in Gramps' voice as he said, "I knew it. That's the well we drilled." Gramps wouldn't say anything else, except "We'll see how it works out for Trish, Mike."

CHAPTER SEVENTEEN

Saying Goodbye

Lisa and Trish would spend Thursday night at Gran's and move their clothes to the new apartment on Friday morning.

The house was quiet, with everyone else asleep, when Gran came into Mike's room and sat on the bed. She seemed reluctant to speak. Finally, she said, "Mike, do you realize there is only one night left before you go home?"

"That can't be right, Gran. Mom said I could stay a little over three weeks."

"Where's your plane ticket?"

Mike opened the desk drawer, and sure enough the flight to Midland left at 10:30 A.M. on Saturday. He couldn't believe the time had gone so fast.

Gran rose and kissed him. "We'll call your folks tomorrow night and be sure they are home."

After Gran left the room, Mike lay in bed and thought about his parents. His mother had gone to Seattle with his dad on a business trip. They should be home by now. Mike had known the time here was almost gone, but he wished he could stay a little longer. So many things had happened. The time had slipped away.

Trish and Lisa gathered their things together the next morning. Plastic bags protected the new clothes. Lisa finished putting a load in the back of the truck when Stacy McInnis walked into the yard.

"Hi, Lisa," she said shyly.

"Hi. Mom and I are moving to our new apartment."

Stacy came closer. "Do you need help?"

"I think we have everything. There isn't much to move."

Stacy stood there awkwardly. Finally, she said, "I guess you are busy." She turned to leave.

"Stacy, wait. Would you like to ride over to the place with us? See where I live?"

Stacy's eyes lit up. "Sure."

"Get in the truck. Mom will be right out."

Trish looked blank when Lisa told her Stacy wanted to see their apartment. Lisa explained, "She's new here, Mom. Maybe we can be friends."

"Oh. All right. Good idea, Lisa."

Trish turned to Gramps and Gran after Lisa had gone outside. "I should tell you I insisted Bob go to the VA hospital again for drug and alcohol addiction. If he won't, he can't live with us any longer."

Gramps could hardly refrain from saying something, but Gran stepped on his toes hard.

Trish threw her arms around Gran. "Thanks so much, Mrs. Shannon," and giving Gramps a hug, "and Mr. Shannon for all your help. You don't know how much it means to Lisa and me."

Outside, Mike opened the truck door for Lisa. She scooted onto the seat next to Stacy and said, "See you later, Mike."

Mike watched the truck until it disappeared from sight. He walked slowly into the house and sat down in the living room. He didn't notice Gran until she spoke.

"The house already seems empty without Trish and Lisa, even if they weren't here very long."

Mike didn't answer but rose and went back to his room.

He began to go over the research notes. He thought of all the things that had happened — of Scotty, Bobby, B. J., and Sam. Most of all, he thought of Lisa and how he hated to leave. He would like to stay and have Lisa for his girl.

He went to the closet and took down his carry-on bag.

After placing the research notes carefully in the bottom of the bag, he left it on the desk with his plane ticket.

Gran still sat in the living room. She hated to see the summer visit end. Rousing herself, she asked, "Do you want to do anything special this evening?"

Sitting on the arm of her chair, Mike answered, "I guess not. I need to tell everyone goodbye."

"Gramps thought maybe we could have the three of us here tonight—just family."

"All right. Whatever you and Gramps want to do."

Gran rose from the chair, and suddenly Mike stood and put his arms around her. "You and Gramps are the best grandparents a guy could have, and I love you."

Mike could see tears on her eyelashes when he released her. Patting him on the shoulder, she almost ran from the room.

Suddenly, Mike remembered what his dad had told him one time: "Son, when things are rough, don't sit and feel sorry for yourself. Get up and get busy."

This would be a good time to tell Bobby goodbye.

Knocking on Burton's door, he smelled cookies baking. Mrs. Burton, an apron tied around her waist and flour on her hands, opened the door.

"Oh hi, Mike." She stood aside. "Come in. Bobby's mowing the backyard."

Mike returned her greeting and walked through the kitchen and out the back door. Bobby had shut off the mower and was emptying the grass bag into a large, plastic-lined trash can.

Seeing Mike, he laid the bag on the ground. He came closer and Mike could see the sweat running down his cheeks. He wiped it off with a towel stuck into the waistband of his shorts and sat down on the back steps.

Mike sat beside him and said, "I've come to say goodbye, Bobby."

"Goodbye? Why? Do you have to go home, already?"

"Yeah, the plane leaves in the morning."

"It doesn't seem like you've been here very long. Can you go with us this evening? Dad is taking me to a ballgame."

"I'd like to, but Gran and Gramps want me to spend the last night with them. We have to phone my folks to be sure they are back home."

Mike tried not to think about it being a year before he would see Bobby again.

He asked, "Do you know anything about Sam or B. J.? I wanted to tell them goodbye."

"Sam's gone for the weekend. I don't know about B. J."

Mike shook Bobby's hand. "Bye, man. Until next time."

"Come back if you can before next summer, Mike, and thanks for helping me the night someone tried to break into my house."

Mike patted him on the shoulder and went through the yard gate without looking back.

Scotty stood in front of Gramps' house. "Your grandmother told me you were leaving tomorrow."

"That's right."

"Could you go on the route with me one last time?"

"I can go this afternoon, but Gran wants me to stay here this evening."

"See you about three, then," Scotty said and started home.

Mike called B. J. on the phone. It was a short conversation. The boys said goodbye, and Mike hung up and went into the kitchen to help Gran with lunch.

Gran wanted to buy Mike a shirt for school, so they went shopping in the afternoon. The clock chimed 2:30 when they came back into the house. Mike told Gran he was going with Scotty on the route.

Scotty on the red bike and Mike on the blue one pedaled to the news building. Parking the bikes, Scotty led the way to the circulation department, where boys were rolling the daily paper and securing it with a rubber band. Mike helped to fill Scotty's bag with the rolled papers.

With Scotty in the lead and throwing papers, the boys soon came to the apartment complex where Lisa lived.

Scotty threw the paper on the small front porch just as Lisa came out the door. Turning to Mike, he said, "She must have known you'd be with me today." Without waiting for an answer, he rode on, calling over his shoulder, "See you later."

Mike and Lisa sat on the porch in the shade. He could hear music softly playing.

"Mom bought me a little radio for my room," Lisa said.

"Good. Lisa, I have to leave in the morning. Gran wants me to be home tonight, so I guess this is goodbye."

"Oh, Mike."

"I know, but will you write to me?"

"Yes. Mike, you mean more to me than any other boy."

"Same goes for me, Lisa."

"What time are you leaving?"

"At ten-thirty."

"From the airport?"

"Yes. Gramps will take me out there."

Mike stood up, took Lisa's hand, and drew her to her feet. Suddenly, he kissed her on the lips, turned, and ran to the bike.

Looking back, he saw Lisa standing there with her fingers pressed to her lips. As his eyes misted with tears, Mike became very angry with himself. He shook his head to clear his eyes and rode as fast as he could pedal to Gramps'.

Jumping off the bike, he entered the house, went to his room, closed the door, and threw himself on the bed. Exhausted, he fell asleep.

A soft knock at the door wakened him. Gran stood there. "Mike, Gramps wants to take us to the Red Lobster for dinner."

Mike rubbed his eyes. "All right, Gran. Be ready in a few minutes."

The seafood dinner was very good, and afterward, Gramps said he wanted to buy Mike something before he left. They went to the mall and shopped in several of the stores.

Back home, Gran mentioned calling Midland. "You call,

Mike. I suspect your mother and dad would like to hear from you."

His mother's voice sounded so good when she said, "Hello."

"Mom?"

"Yes, Mike."

"I'll be home tomorrow."

"I know. We're looking forward to having you back home. We've missed you. Dad and I will be at the airport. Anything else?"

"I guess not."

"We love you, Mike."

"Me, too, Mom."

"See you tomorrow." She hung up.

CHAPTER EIGHTEEN

Headed for Home

Mike thought some of the guys would show up the next morning, but they didn't. Gran helped him get his things packed, and they started for the airport about 9:30.

His large bag checked and the carry-on in hand, Mike and his grandparents walked to the waiting area. Mike couldn't believe his eyes. There were Bobby and his parents, B. J., Scotty, Trish, and Lisa. Everyone began to talk at once.

Trish said it best. "We couldn't let you leave, Mike, without telling you what your visit has meant to all of us. Thanks a million, and maybe we can repay you sometime." She kissed him, and hugs followed from everyone else. Bobby's dad patted him several times on the back.

The call for his flight came over the intercom and then the announcement that passengers could board. Gramps' hands were trembling a little as he shook hands with Mike. Gran had some tears in her eyes.

Mike walked through the gate and climbed the steps into the plane. Seating himself near a window, he looked out and saw them all standing there at the fence. He watched as the plane took off until they were lost in the distance. Airborne, he headed for home.

Many thoughts went through Mike's head on the flight — all the summer visit had meant to him, the friends, the problems, the research. The visit had been a good one, and in many ways he was sorry to see it end. But now, he was on his way back to Mom and Dad and school.

CHAPTER NINETEEN

Successful Summer

At home, Mike's life settled quickly into the old routine. He told his mom and dad about the summer visit — about Trish and Lisa and Bob, about how much Lisa meant to him, about how Gran would help Trish and Lisa. His mom said maybe Lisa and Trish could come to Midland sometime during the holidays when Gramps and Gran were there.

Mike's eyes shone. "That would be great if they could come. I know you and Dad would like them."

School started. Mike studied the research notes and decided to build the pump jack. With his school work, football, and basketball, he would have to start on the project early.

He spent many hours perfecting the small model. Built from a lightweight metal resembling aluminum, and with a battery-powered DC motor, the little model took shape.

Proudly, Mike showed it to Gramps and Gran when they came, and he showed it again when Trish and Lisa visited during the Christmas holiday.

Bob had gone to the VA hospital for psychiatric counseling and treatment for drug and alcohol abuse. Lisa told Mike privately she hoped he wouldn't come back. Mike knew after the holidays were over and everyone had gone back to Kilgore that his feelings for Lisa were still the same. She remained his first and only girl, and they would keep in contact with each other.

The Science Fair occupied most of his free time. At his dad's suggestion, he added the pipe running from the small model over to a storage tank to make the display as authentic as possible.

Sponsored by the Math and Science Booster Club to increase interest in those two fields, Expo '92 was limited to the Midland Independent School District and would be held at Midland College the last of February. Entered in the Earth Science Division, Mike set up his display among many others. He had made posters using print shop software on a computer at school to mount on a trifold cardboard stand, which he placed behind the miniature model.

The whole thing looked good to Mike when he stood back and surveyed the months of research. On the trifold the title was simply stated as "A PUMP JACK." Under "PURPOSE" he wrote: "To bring up oil from non-flowing wells." He explained the difference between the use of a Christmas tree and the pump jack. The other space gave an explanation of how the pump jack worked.

Mike received a first-place ribbon for his exhibit.

Less than six weeks later, in April, he put the exhibit up again. This time it was at the University of Texas–Permian Basin for the Regional Science Fair. Again he received first place.

Before the fair ended, an oil company executive made a point to speak to Mike. He said his company would like to keep in touch when Mike was in high school. This was in case Mike decided to pursue a career in earth sciences, maybe in the field of engineering.

The fairs over, Mike's dad suggested he call Gramps and thank him for his help the past summer. From this phone call Mike learned several things.

Gramps said, "Trish has been contacted by a company tracking down mineral rights on a six-hundred-forty-acre lease. You remember, Mike, the old pump jack we found in that field?"

"Yes, sir."

"Long Trusts of Kilgore wants to pursue some deeper

drilling into some of the old capped wells. Trish's land is within this lease, and she owns most of the mineral rights."

"Didn't your folks own that land, Gramps?"

"No. Clarks owned the place. The older Clark was Trish's grandfather, and when her parents died, Trish inherited the place. My folks rented the place while they were all away from here."

Gramps continued, "Trish will have to get a few legal papers signed proving she owns the land."

Mike could tell by Gramps' voice he wasn't pleased when he said, "Another thing. Trish has let Bob move back home with the agreement he shape up or —"

Gramps didn't finish the sentence, and Mike could hear Gran saying something.

Smiling to himself, Mike said, "Gramps, thanks for all your help. Will you and Gran look out for Trish and Lisa? Tell Lisa I'll see her before too long when I come to visit for the summer."

Gramps laughed. "How can we help but look out for them when they adopted us as parents and grandparents?"

"Okay. Thanks again, Gramps. I love you and Gran.

"We know that, boy. We'll see you before too long."

Lying in bed that night, Mike thought back over the last months and what the research had proved. The science project couldn't have gone better, Bobby's and Scotty's problems had been solved, and above all, he now had Lisa.

He didn't know about Sam and B. J. Maybe more research would be necessary there.

Glossary

(These terms vary from time to time and place to place.)

anticline – a fold with strata sloping downward.

boomers – best mechanics.

cable tool drilling – drilling with solid steel cylindrical bit working vertically in the hole and activated by a walking beam and steel line.

cap rock – layer of clay or salt which prevents leakage of oil to surface.

chalk – soft variety of limestone.

Christmas tree – valves and gauges at the top of the casing in a flowing well for control of oil and gas.

circulating for samples – procedure to stop drilling while the mud pressure and circulation bring fresh rock cuttings from the bottom of the hole to the shale shaker for inspection and oil show.

circulation – continuous cycling of mud stream through the drill pipe back to the surface.

derrick – framework of steel which supports drill pipe. (The drill pipe carries drill bit, which drills through layers of rock.)

dragged up – going to drag up or quit; moving from one rig to another or one drill site to another.

drill bit – bits with three or four rollers with long or short teeth to bite into rock. (Long teeth are used for soft rock and short teeth for hard rock; a bit studded with diamonds is for very hard rock.)

drill mud — substance made of chemicals, clay, water, and sometimes oil in place of water. (Pumped inside drill pipe, it goes through holes in the bit and cools drill bit; forced back to surface outside drill pipe.)

drill pipe casing — lengths of steel pipe cemented into place to line drill hole.

drug you up — got fired by foreman.

flanged up — job is finished.

flooding — to inject water into a depleted well to force any remaining oil to another well for production.

gas flare — gas being burned off through pipe to separate it from crude oil in the drill hole.

kelly — hollow, forty-foot stem attached to drill pipe and turned by the rotary table during drilling.

lost circulation — rotary drilling hazard when mud is lost in porous or cavernous formation and fails to circulate back to pits.

main fairway — lane running the length of the oil field.

roughnecks — men on a drilling rig.

roustabouts — men who maintain and work on wells.

salt dome — bed of salt wedged into layers of rock.

spud in — to start drilling.

tool pusher — man in charge of all drilling operations; drilling supervisor.

wild cat well — well drilled in new area after survey.

Woodbine sand — named for small community where it was discovered near Dallas. A water-bearing layer of sand that came out on the surface and supplied water to Dallas. This layer is where the oil was found in the East Texas Oil Field.

Bibliography

Berger, Bill D., and Kenneth E. Anderson. *Modern Petroleum: A Basic Primer of the Industry.* 2nd ed. Tulsa OK: PennWell Publishing Co., 1981. (Picture of pump jack from this edition.)

Hawkes, Nigel. *Oil.* New York: Gloucester Press, 1985.

McHaney, Helen Ray. "The East Texas Oil Field." Thesis presented to faculty of Stephen F. Austin State College in partial fulfillment of the requirements for degree in master of arts, July 1953.

Nixon, Hershell, and Joan Lowery. *Oil and Gas from Fossils to Fuels.* New York: Harcourt Brace Jovanovich, 1977.

Potter, Neil. *Oil.* Morristown, NJ: Silver Burdett Co., 1980.

Rice, Dale. *Energy from Fossil Fuels.* Milwaukee, WI: Raintree Publishers, 1983.